The Gift of Fear

irrational tales

MATT FINUCANE

It is not mere blood that feeds this lust I feel now to tenant you, this craving for an intimacy that years will not stale. My truest feast lies in compelling you to feed in that way.

Michael Shea, "The Autopsy"

CONTENTS

COMPLAINT FROM THE OTHER WORLD

So I'm standing by this wall, right, waiting for my girlfriend and trying to enjoy the afternoon sun.

At least, I think she was my girlfriend – in theory, you know what I mean, but less so in actual disposition. Paying attention, showing up, being nice, stuff like that.

I'm trying to enjoy the sunshine, which I can't feel, and trying not to bite my nails, which I can't feel.

Then out of the crowd she comes, and I call out 'Barb,' but not too loud, and maybe she doesn't hear me: instead of stopping or even looking round, she passes on by.

Not even a pause – there she goes, Barbara Witt, off into the crowd again: walking confidently, slipping between the jostle, then gone. I notice everyone else is avoiding my eye too, maybe to spare my embarrassment. As snubs go, that was pretty damn public.

But then I can't blame her.

Nobody's looking at me – her or anyone else – because I'm embedded in the wall.

I'm flat, featureless, less than a shadow; just a darker spot like an outline of a person that someone spray-painted on there a long time ago, nearly effaced by fumes and rain.

I'm embedded, and while I can see, and hear and call out very quietly when I've got the strength, I can't move. I'm lodged in a thin film between the bricks and the air, the bulk (bulk? Ha) of what used to be my substance bound to the bricks.

Now if you'll bear with me, I'll explain why. I'd stop whispering, but I can't; it's been a draining sort of a day and I don't have the energy to talk louder. I should add – and I'm sorry I didn't sooner, I'm not normally rude but I'm under stress – that I really, really appreciate you stopping to listen. Not many would, obviously, so this is a real pleasure. Thank you. I mean that: thank you. Don't worry, it won't take long – I know it's getting late now. You must be very brave, standing there in the dark listening to a wall. I wish I could see you better.

Anyway, the brief version:

At one point, believe it or not – but why wouldn't you, you've never actually met her – Barbara was in a very bad way, in a lot of trouble. Family, stuff, childhood, you know. Bad stuff that came back up in a big ugly ball soon after we became an item, and by then I really, really wanted to help.

First it was drugs and drink; there was some kind of underlying depression thing she was trying to self-medicate, but then she managed to cut all that out – not easy, but she managed. Looking at her today, you'd understand why. A strong, strong woman.

But. While she was still unstable after the shock of coming off the Valium, Citalopram, Librium and Zopiclone (and that's just the legally-prescribed stuff: I'm not even going to mention the other things she was taking), plus the wine and vodka, she got involved with these people. She was fragile, she was emotionally all over the place: good meat for them, in other words.

We weren't getting on too well at this point – after all, I did my best but she wasn't the easiest to live with: it was mainly the insomnia that made her so bad-tempered, I think, that and the panic attacks. Mood swings, you know. So I gave her some space, said I'd some back, and did.

By then she'd joined this weird group. Not a cult, well not technically, but weird.

Pagans, they'd probably call themselves. Just to make themselves sound all New Age and nature-loving and harmless. Which they clearly weren't. I'd best not tell you their name, but trust me. They're a lot more dangerous than they look.

Moving along, I got her away from them – surprisingly easily, they were very nice about it in fact, the underhanded bastards – and we went through another few rocky weeks. Difficult, but we got there in the end and we still cared about eachother.

Then I started getting these weird letters, and emails, and texts, from these cult people. How did they get my details, I wondered, and of course Barb and I had a screaming row and I all but accused her of giving them my contacts. I didn't quite, but she picked up the thought as it crossed my mind and was disregarded, the way women do, you know, and chose to take it badly. Understandable, but still.

So I did something I still regret. Because now I'll never be able to make it up to her. I called her a two-faced, manipulative, ungrateful witch and walked out. Yes, witch; I told you this group was weird.

And we've not spoken since. You can see why.

I went and stayed with a friend, and one night when I was going to the local off-licence for supplies, they caught me.

Three or four of them, it all happened too quickly to tell.

They did their thing, and now here I am, and here I've been for months – for I don't know how long.

Enough time to get very bored with the contents of my mind, such as it is.

And I hoped, today: I've been saving my energy, and today, she'll walk past on her way to work, and I'll call out, and she'll see me. Maybe she can help me, maybe not. Just to see me would be enough, but no such luck – on she goes. Probably got a new boyfriend by now too.

Sorry, didn't mean to get maudlin.

But it's good to find someone who'll listen. Thanks again.

…You are still there, aren't you? My eyes aren't what they were, yes, bad joke, but I'm getting a bit nervous again. I don't want to find out I've been talking to a lamp-post for the last half hour.

Hello?

A CURSE IN ANY LANGUAGE

William Burroughs wrote that the word is a virus. He was foolish and wrong about a lot of things, but in this he was correct.

My girlfriend was always into trying new modes, testing herself, learning new languages. In a quiet unforced way, one that would have made her a resourceful and useful person someday, an asset to the world. It was there to see in her kindness and percipience, all so near finding an outlet.

Yes, a real tangible asset to this fucking world. If she'd lived.

She died at twenty-two in a way so horrible it makes me want to run out into the streets and stab every person I see. The couples, the singles, young, old, male, female... To destroy everyone and everything.

And perhaps I can.

I wouldn't even need that knife, nor any other weapon you'd understand.

When this nauseating rage achieves a balance with its polar opposite – of not caring at all – I may well try to find out.

My conscience is clear, though – I'll leave it somewhere, maybe somewhere it won't be found, and let chance do the rest.

We'll see.

It began and ended with one of her new languages.

I got back to the flat and found her home unexpectedly, with a pile of books.

'You okay?' I said, assuming she'd left early with a bug or cold;

she was a dedicated worker. I will happily make her former office my first target.

They gave her the book. Why? And what was it doing there? But that's irrelevant.

'Yeah, fine thanks. Look at this.' She held out the book, open at two yellowed pages of scrawled handwriting. 'They were clearing out the basement archives and found this old thing. Nobody could figure out what it was so they let me take it.'

'Any idea what it is?'

'I'm not sure – it's like... like someone trying to invent a new language. Here, see what you reckon.'

I see her like this often, offering me the weapon.

[..........]

That's what the hose is for, yes, and the drains. No mess.

Hard work, but could be worse.

Never. I've made it a point of pride never to call for help, partly as I'm not sure if the panic button works anymore. Not been serviced that I'm aware of, cutbacks and that.

Still – I expect that's partly why you're here. The Man from the Ministry, as they say.

Wouldn't be time to get to the intercom, good grief no.

Don't look so worried; still, you look very young to be an administrator. Fast track, I expect, clever. You won't have seen the sharp end of it before.

Worry not – I can always tell when we're due for another one: instinct. It'll be a while.

Been a quiet few days, actually. I feel nice and rested, good for staying alert.

Sometimes it gets very hectic.

They come trooping through that door like I don't know what.

All sorts. You never know what to expect, varies enormously.

Some could, yes. Others could never pass for human, not in a million years. Have we got a million years, do you think?

No but seriously. Horrible, some of them. You've just had lunch, haven't you.

Stop worrying. There's the five minute warning, and look at the door – look how big the hinges are. Weighs a couple of tons at least.

…Yes, some of them can be rather nasty.

Well, I was reading in the news about those scientists, the argument, about whether these are really living creatures at all. Bit complicated to follow – especially rushing about with work – but maybe you can explain it to me.

Well, not many can. I mean, it's a funny kind of problem.

I think it was bacteria, that was the example. Something similar. Some sort of ocean microbe, or was it mineral, mixed with pollution and started moving about. The other idea sounds like bollocks: something to do with a book that infected people, some fella started spreading it around. Heard that one?

Imagine that, the door opens and out comes fuck knows what, all dripping from the sea. Because of a book. Nah.

Of course I've got regrets, but it's good money, not that Municipal Currency rubbish: I can keep a nice full fridge.

Back to business. This is the modulator, yes. Special frequency, harmless to humans but blows them apart. All a bit mucky, hence the drains. One way of telling if they're real people or not, I suppose.

My apologies – bad joke. It can be upsetting if they look more or less normal, yes, but you never forget what'll happen to you if they touch you.

[………..]

It was a camping holiday with a girl I met at a festival.

'Never mind that, she was a sweet Euro-babe and I wanted to get in bed with her but wasn't sure she was up for it. She was a space cadet, leylines and earth-lights, UFOs – magic mushrooms, crappy trance music, that kind of thing. Wanted to re-create the festival vibe, so we went camping in some fields in the middle of nowhere. I forget if we were looking for ghosts or flying saucers.'

'The girl's name was Kelli Nyquist,' said one of the scientists.

'Yes, and I realised she didn't fancy me after all, so I drank all her apple gin and passed out. Woke up for a piss in the middle of the night and went into the forest. You know, maybe a puke or a dump too.'

'And that's where you found the device,' said one of the labcoats.

'Yep, that's where I found the "device", if you mean that

6

book.' Scott realised something was wrong with him; he kept talking to anchor himself as his vision began to flicker and cut out at the edges. 'You know all this already. So what's the story?' They must have slipped him something in his water; any minute now he was going to keel over in this chair and get away from the overpowering smell of these men's mingling aftershaves. The smell filled his head like the light, which was growing speckled and heavy. 'I found the book just lying there... So I picked it up and it felt a bit strange, like it wanted to be read – I'm not rambling am I, except I am, and jeez I need to lie down...'

One of the scientists knelt before him, but not close. 'How long now since you've been exposed? What symptoms have you noticed?'

'Err... Help me out here.'

'Unusual rashes or skin discolorations, altered diet, anything like that. And did you read the book?'

Scott was now canted at an angle that showed him the underside of the plastic chairs facing him and the shiny shoes of his questioners. He giggled. 'Come to think of it, yes. Funny thing...'

'What?'

'The last half of it was missing. The pages had been torn out.'

His concentration was shading away into faintness, his grip on consciousness softly prised away as a grey bubble settled over him. Through his fattened tongue, he asked, 'Did I mention I gave the book to Kelli?'

He just had time to enjoy their looks of confused fear before the toxin shrank him to nothing.

LUCKY BLEEDER

Stevie Mitchell was caught – and paralysed – between two powerful emotions.

On the one hand, he couldn't believe his luck.

On the other and more potently, he was terrified. The barricade on his door looked more ramshackle with each shouting, hammering attack; it wouldn't hold for much longer.

As a getaway, the window was out of the question – too high up, and there were noises in the carpark as chaotic and animalistic as the ones up and down the hallway.

Jesus God, he asked himself again when things had quieted down a little and he was able to think – how could things have changed literally overnight, in such a... Such a... He wasn't sure whether he liked it or not.

After all, he was a late starter: a virgin.

A chilling shriek from somewhere made him twitch and he realised he probably wasn't that keen. He was well-read enough to fake a conversation with the sort of girls who were into literature and shit, myths, and he knew the gist of those stories – the ones about ancient Greek men being torn apart by maddened women – Bacchae? Maenads?

If he went outside now, that was exactly what could happen. Conversation was redundant.

Every woman on the campus had turned into a ravening sex-fiend; every man too. Everyone.

Everyone except him.

'What the fuck's going on?' he said, but quietly, in case anyone was waiting outside.

The television in the corner was on with the sound down. News and all other programmes had been replaced by blurry, whirling footage of naked bodies grappling and swaying in TV studios, shops, streets, everywhere.

He changed the channel and saw something that frightened him even more: a park.

He saw a montage of rutting squirrels, pigeons, swans, lakes seething with copulating fish and frogs – dogs with cats, owls with litter bins, a fox with something that might have been a tortoise. The view bounced to an unsteady rhythm as the cameraman masturbated.

It could be to do with something he'd read in one of the papers sopping up beer in the student union.

Something about the planets coming into an odd conjunction and amplifying these cosmic rays scientists were worried about. He didn't really care. He wanted his mother.

She'd get him out of here.

He fumbled with the sticky keypad of his mobile. 'Mam? Please pick up, it's Stevie. I'm in real trouble –'

The phone was answered, but a crash and a choked cry outside made him jump miserably and he missed whatever the reply might have been.

'Please, it's urgent – pick up or text me, whatever, I really really need you to come get me right now. In the car. Please!'

There was a moment's listening silence on the other end of the line, then a loud clunk.

'…Mam?'

'Uh uh uh uh UHHH!'

'Come on, stop it,' Stevie was close to tears now.

'It's okay Stevie love, we'll come get you. We miss you baby.' She gave a horrible mindless scream of pleasure.

Stevie hurled the phone under the bed.

He sat on the bed and began to shiver. He was in London. His parents lived in Preston.

Furry moaning noises crept from under the bed until he snatched the phone back and stamped it into a wafer of circuits.

As the door began to buckle and shatter a few minutes later, he realised this might have been a foolish move.

The flimsy barricade flew apart. In a moment when he felt the fulcrum of his personality teeter – How could he consider such a thing? – he looked at the smashed glass of the lamp he'd bought in Camden Lock and considered its viability as a cutting weapon.

But by then, a girl he didn't recognise had stormed into the room.

She was attractive, which was some small consolation once she attacked him, tearing and biting.

The fact he couldn't get it up and then puked with fear was what made her keep on biting until he was dead.

HOUNDED

'Once upon a time there was a lovely little puppy called Wattles. One day as he walked through the forest, he smelt a delicious meat pie, cooling on the window ledge of a cottage…'

Seeing the look on his son's face, Hugh Sand stopped reading. 'Well no, perhaps not.' He leafed through the contents pages of the old story-book. 'Let's see if we can find another one…'

'I've heard all the rest already, Daddy,' said Toby.

'Well, would you like to give that one a try anyway? Go on.'

Toby twisted in bed, fidgeting at the cuffs of his bright red pyjama top. 'No, Daddy. Please don't read that one.'

The hysterical edge on his son's voice added pressure to Sand's headache. More sharply than he'd intended, he said, 'There's nothing scary about it. Don't be so silly. When I was your age –' He tailed off, realizing he had no idea how he'd felt at Toby's age; the boy was only six, after all.

'There's a doggy in it, Daddy.'

'I know,' said Sand more gently, 'but it's a nice doggy. And it's ever such a funny story.' He hoped.

'But it's a *doggy*.'

Suddenly he was tired of humouring the boy. He'd had a long – a hideously long – and stressful day, he was exhausted, and this nonsense had been going on for weeks. He stood up, clapping the book shut. 'Right. If you can't be a bit more sensible about this, it's time to go to sleep. Goodnight.'

11

He just managed not to slam the door after switching off the lamp beside his son's creasing, wilfully miserable face. Why couldn't the boy be a bit more cooperative?

A few seconds later he felt a wave of guilt and shame that pushed him up against the wall, eyes closed. Then he opened them and looked around the gloomy hallway – at the too-large house they'd bought in a daze of complacency that now appalled him. He wondered again how he was ever going to finish paying for it. The recession had doused any hope of the promotion he'd banked on, and now he had to work insane hours just to heat and light the miserable place. Leaving aside the money problem, how in God's name could he ever have thought the three of them could make such a mouldy old museum their home? Added to his remorse at being so harsh with Toby, the thought brought depression rolling over him, and hard as it was to credit, his headache cranked up even higher; soon he'd be half-blind with it. He'd been about to go apologize; in his present state he might just make things worse. He stumbled away from the wall, groping along dim corridors to the bathroom.

Naomi came in as he was ransacking the cabinet and drawers for painkillers. She watched him in the mirror, obviously reluctant to speak.

'Well?' he said thickly.

'I might have some aspirin in my bag if you want them.'

'Why didn't you say so? Go get them, please.' And for fuck's sake hurry up.

Some time later, he was able to sit in the lounge and think about a small brandy before bed. The TV was on with sound down low, but he knew Naomi was only using it to hide constant peripheral glances at him. Before she could raise the next, inevitable question, he attacked the subject in a voice he was careful to keep calm and even. 'I'm afraid it was the same rigamarole tonight.'

'About that dog?'

'Yes, the dog, the... yes dear, *that* dog.'

'The one we "inherited"?' She spoke the final word with self-conscious lightness.

'As I just bloody said. *Yes*. Jesus.'

'Please don't take that tone with me.'

Ignoring her – the way he felt, her words sounded too close to provocation – he said, 'It's just an old wives' tale. And if I get my hands on the old wife, or more likely ignorant little shit who told him, I'll seriously injure them.'

'You still think someone at school said it. Makes sense, I suppose.'

'Of course it does. Look, we've been over this before: there's no other way he could've been exposed to that… stupid story. Those inbred swede-bashers probably did it on purpose to scare the new boy. The townie.' He grimaced. 'And when I think of the rosy picture they painted at HQ: "you'll love relocating, you can sit out the recession, in fact you can oversee the downsizing on-site, the factory staff'll hate your guts as you decimate their jobs, but at least yours is safe – and you'll get away from London." Why? Why did we want that? I can't even remember now. Oh yes, and "you'll be hands-on, right in the thick of it," they said. We're in the thick of something, alright.'

'Get off it, Hugh. We both wanted a change. And Toby…'

'Would've been better off staying put in that not-really-so-bad school in Peckham Rye. I've come to hate the countryside so much. The mud, the boredom, the prejudice…'

'Everyone was lovely to that Albanian family when they stayed in the hostel.'

'I meant prejudice as regards this house, dear. "Doctor Grayner's house. The wizard's house." I mean that's got to be, what, two hundred years back? The way some of those old soaks at the Blacksmiths Arms carry on you'd think it was built yesterday.' He looked round the damp, brownish room. 'In fact I wish it had been. Save us a lot of hassle. Have you seen the state of the guttering since last week?'

'A child did disappear here once,' said Naomi quietly.

'Speaking of dogs, that estate agent certainly sold us a pup.' Then her remark registered. 'Yes, thirty years ago. He probably fell through a rotten floor. Besides, they had paedophiles back then too, you know.' Seeing her lips thinning, he quickly waved a hand to negate the remark. 'Bad taste, sorry. But same thing: ancient history. All very tragic, but I can't *believe* these yokels are still talking about it – and passing it on to their kids, which is worse.'

'Nobody's asking you to believe anything. The thing is, Toby does.'

'I mean, look at it – poky little thing. Hardly a decent kennel for Satan's mastiff.'

The fireplace was small, sooty and unimpressive, with a black mantel and a fine silt of ash ingrained on the tiles. At some point, it had been bricked up.

Naomi made no reply; she gave him a flat look and walked out of the room.

He sighed, counted to ten, then got up to follow. As he passed the fireplace more closely, something caught his eye, making him scowl. A stray breeze down the chimney sometimes sifted through the crumbling brickwork blocking off the flue. The patina of ash never seemed to go away, and the breeze traced shapes in it that from a certain angle could look like anything at all.

Sand stared at the smudges like paw-prints in the fireplace for a moment, then scuffed them away with his heel.

In the bedroom corridor, he could hear Naomi's voice in Toby's room, low and measured.

He waited for her, and when she emerged her look of vindicated relief made him untense a little. 'He okay now?' Sand whispered.

'Yes, no thanks to you. You really are a sod sometimes, snapping at him like that.' But she sounded too reassured to be argumentative.

'Oh, he told you, did he?' Sand's headache flared again for a moment, then he made his tone conciliatory. 'I'm sorry. I've had a bastard day and he just wouldn't settle.' A thought came to him, a way of appealing to her. 'And he'll get a complex about it if we encourage him. I was only trying to talk him out of it.' Which was just about true, at a stretch.

'That's ridiculously old-fashioned thinking,' she said, but went on, 'let's discuss it when we're less tired.'

When would that be? He grunted agreement anyway; off the hook, then.

They went to their bedroom and silently got ready for sleep.

Sand watched without comment as Naomi dug into her bedside cabinet and produced the Temazepam she'd somehow wheedled out of their GP before they left London. She popped a near-overdose into her mouth, chased it with water and rolled over, switching off her lamp. In seconds she'd be unconscious all through the night, Sand thought enviously. What was she going to do when she ran out, though? She was hitting them pretty hard and their new GP, unlike the previous, didn't fancy her. What then? Well, we're all on borrowed time here, he thought – borrowed everything, in fact.

His headache showed no sign of lifting.

He lay in the dark for a long time, thoughts tangling and ripping apart bloodily. This huge house, this wretched town; it had all been such a mistake. Where was he to find the money? His new colleagues in admin were standoffish and had made it plain he was last in line for any kind of preferment; Naomi with all her qualifications had only been able to find part-time work in a cake shop. And Toby was unhappy, hated the place – ungrateful tyke, he was making it ten times as difficult; was turning into a proper little mummy's boy. No, that wasn't fair, he was just out of his element and jumpy, was having nightmares. All over some fairy-tale, the stupid little... Relax, Sand ordered himself.

Still, it was hardly a relaxing situation for any of them, was it? And they'd thought they were escaping the stresses and strains of their unbalanced city existence. Oh, the peal of irony – like bells – or jingling coins, a sweet sound... Sand fell asleep.

In his dream, Sand was in an indeterminate space that seemed alternately vast and claustrophobically small, its walls or horizons composed of some flickering black stuff shot through with flashes of red.

A presence, an immensely heavy ball of blood and hair, hung somewhere before and above him; he felt it observing him, radiating its massive impulses into his bones. He realised it was trying to communicate and felt a kind of fearful gratitude which he knew it could sense. The beats thudding through him took on a crude but understandable pattern; it was offering him a gift. Before he could ask what this gift or bargain was, some base part of him had reacted with eagerness and awe – had signified his acceptance.

There was a shift in the atmosphere, a discordance, and with an acute lurch of fright Sand knew he'd chosen wrongly – disastrously. He tried to catch at the presence, signal to it and take his decision back before finding out what was expected of him in

15

return. But the presence had gone, leaving him alone in the red-black landscape.

A dog appeared beside him. It was large and sleek, its ears bat-wing points, its short fur a strange blue-white. It looked up at him with wide blue eyes full of innocent contempt. As Sand gazed at it, it chuckled and whispered something in a human voice too low for him to make out. Then it slipped away into the darkness.

The dream changed, and Sand found himself in the lounge at night. He was waiting in front of the fireplace. The dog leapt out from it at him, and now its fur was haloed with crackling white light, its eyes whirling silver coins.

A shrill scream bolted him awake.

He launched himself out of bed and through the door while Naomi blinked her way out of sedation, groggily questioning.

Toby's room was empty, then there was another scream from downstairs.

As Sand kicked the lounge door aside, he heard a fading canine chuckle.

The room was empty; in the fireplace, somehow fused into the bricks behind the grate as though caught there, was a chewed-looking scrap of a bright red pyjama sleeve.

THE UN-EXPLORERS

It started with the Golem, I think. Or maybe it was earlier than that. After everything that's happened, I can't remember how the idea originated, exactly, only how it got so complicated and strange.

I'd meant this to be a dry, sort of scholarly account of what we found, but I see now that's not going to work: might even be less convincing to the uninitiated. Besides, none of us were exactly geniuses, as should become all too clear. So, then...

The real beginning, my beginning anyway, was when my girlfriend left me. I can't honestly blame her – I'd stopped taking my antidepressants because they were making me bloated and dopey, and she just couldn't cope with the mood-swings. This might explain some of what followed; I was in a strange place emotionally and couldn't sleep at all (and I mean *at all*), so lots of very unusual things seemed perfectly reasonable at the time.

The first consequence was that I was rattling around on my own in the flat – a big place out in the suburbs we'd fluked somehow, a house almost – and got lonely. So I invited a friend to stay for a while. And when he suggested inviting someone else, I thought it was a great plan. And when they invited someone in turn, I was delighted: at last I could have all that student-type fun I'd missed out on at the time! The rent was cheap, I'd saved a bit, I was on sick leave – and I was newly single. Party on dude, et-bloody-cetera. So there I was with all the company I could wish for and sometimes more – an ever-changing cast of hangers-on trooped in and out, crashing on the floor, but the core group stayed pretty stable. Initially, at least.

It wasn't some sort of commune, don't get that idea, but it wasn't exactly a dormitory for sober professionals either. My model was the household of Dr Samuel Johnson (whose biography I'd been reading when Stella ran off to her parents). He took in all kinds of needy strays, a real mixed bag, and they lived in chaos in his rickety London home, some of them for years. This was the ideal; the reality was more like a sitcom written by Aleister Crowley (minus the orgies, unfortunately).

None of us was exactly teenaged anymore, but none of us could seem to shed the bad habits and overindulgences we'd contracted when younger – and it's not so cute when you're a pill-gobbling, borderline alcoholic in your mid-thirties. How some of us held down real jobs still mystifies me today.

Other, bigger things mystify me a lot more. That's a cheap way of leading you on, but hey: no point being tasteful. And I'm only being flippant because I'm scared.

Right, I'm going to rattle through this or else I'll lose my nerve and never get it all down. If I had to fix a point where things got serious, it'd be this:

We had a fair-sized patch of garden, screened from the neighbours by trees and overgrown hedges, which sloped steeply downwards into a mass of creepers and nettles. This is where Jerry built the Golem.

Now, we were four emotionally-damaged guys, each of us a little unsteady in their own way – with our revolving-door troupe of parasites sleeping on duvets all over the place – each of us orbiting hopelessly round girls who weren't interested, creative projects never completed, and whatever narcotic we could get our hands on (and of course, the off-licence). We had one rule, though – never interfere with whatever obsession, whatever maggot was fixating any one of us at any given time; if possible, don't even question it. God help us, we thought it was therapeutic.

So we left Jerry to dig up most of the bottom end of the garden, waiting for whatever artistic oddity might result – and when he'd finished, there was the Golem.

It wasn't an actual Golem in the dictionary sense; that's just what we all called it. It wasn't meant to come to life and move around or anything. It was a big, lumpy, manlike shape made of sandy earth, standing on the edge of the pit from which that earth had been excavated. It was a good hot summer, and pretty soon the thing was more or less baked solid – it was hollow, you see. And that was when Jerry showed us the tunnel in the pit wall, a crawlspace he was using to get inside the Golem.

He'd scramble up through the mud and stand inside the earthen suit he'd made, sometimes for hours on end, out there in the heat and silence. It had crude arms hanging at its sides, no legs, a big domed head – and two holes bored in that faceless ball for eyes. Jerry's eyes, looking out over the garden.

We all tried it, of course, but I don't like confined spaces and lasted less than ten minutes – Didier and Ed held out a little longer, but none of us could really see the appeal. Jerry, however, said it put him into a hypnotic state unlike any he'd ever experienced. He said it was like being in a survival suit on a marvellous, unexplored new world – immobilised by incredible atmospheric pressures, but safe within the shell to look out across a glittering landscape bathed in unknown radiations and shot through with colours never seen on Earth.

Personally, I thought he'd just had a touch of heatstroke. That, and he was treating magic mushrooms as one of the major food groups.

So okay, I admit I needled him a bit. He was getting on my nerves by this stage – in fact, he was giving me the creeps. All those long, wordless, trancelike fugues at the kitchen table or wherever – he'd just sit there, staring off into space with a knowing little smirk. He started talking about staking out this new reality he'd discovered, how we could be pioneers, living in our world but simultaneously beyond it, or above it or beneath it, in the "interstitial space".

One evening he was banging on about us becoming "astronauts of the liminal" and I finally snapped. I was trying to watch TV – I forget where the others were and for once we didn't have any camp-followers cluttering up the place – and he was droning on and on like someone who's read far too much J G Ballard. So I broke The Rule.

He was in mid-flow and I said something like, "look, this is all very novel, but you're getting a bit boring on the subject. I don't mind you wandering around the million-hued worlds of your imagination, you've found a new game and I'm happy for you, but do you have to give us a fucking lecture about it all the time?"

Of course, he didn't like that much. Not the rudeness; the bit he objected to was my assertion that he was imagining the whole thing.

So he decided to prove it to us. That's where the trouble started – or deepened. Our big mistake was humouring him: those sulks and those weird, staring silences just got too much. Besides, we somehow knew that if we asked him to leave, the whole swinging bachelor vibe would disintegrate. It was stretched pretty thin by then anyway, but none of us had anything better to do; no real responsibilities, which in a way was great; in another sense, it meant we cared about nothing – and nobody cared about us. We – or I – had turned into exactly the sort of disengaged, directionless middle-class wanker I'd always thought I despised. So maybe this played a part too.

I didn't want our fraying camaraderie to vanish, I didn't want to be left on my own again to face up to my stalled life; but there was also the ratty urge to just say, Fuck it then, and sweep all the cards off the table.

So I thought okay, we'll play along with him, shut him up, help him get it out of his system, maybe have a laugh on the way. It's something to do, after all. The others agreed like the poor stoned fools they were.

DAY ONE

Mental preparation, or "acclimatisation", as Jerry called it. "Bollocks", I called it, but each to their own. We sat in the darkened front room, trying to visualise utter blank nothingness forever. This, according to Jerry, was the shell that had to be pierced, the outer atmosphere, of the co-existent space we were to step into. Once past this "habituation barrier", things should become clearer, he reckoned. This wasn't meditation – it was something less passive, more aggressive and purposeful, than that: or so he said. I read and outgrew a lot of daft books about astral projection in my teens (anything to escape an eventless and friendless existence), and this didn't sound very different. So I got bored, and my attention wandered. Rather than passing through some notional mesh beyond eternity (a deliberate inconsistency that Jerry never quite bothered to explain), my mind fixed on the unpleasant smell in the small room. That was Jerry. In a brilliant piece of method acting, he'd stopped washing, shaving, changing his clothes, eating, sleeping... The very picture of the driven scientist engulfed by his research. Ed and Didier just smelt of skunk and red wine, but that was the ambient odour of the entire flat and I barely noticed it. They were much more into it than I was, by virtue of their suggestible – if not paralysed – mental state. The room was filled by three hoarse, deep, regular breathing cycles, all synchronised. Mine was faster and more pinched, largely because Jerry's own personal atmosphere was making me ill; I hadn't eaten for a couple of days, which didn't help. My low blood sugar probably made my mood irritable and unreceptive too, as I reflected on how little I actually had in common with Jerry – he was Ed's friend really – and felt a growing resentment at how he'd monopolised our time.

This might be what saved me. I didn't get as far in as the others, then or later.

DAY TWO
More of the same. I cornered Ed and Didier when Jerry went for one of his rare toilet breaks, and complained that humouring him was all very well in theory, but hadn't this gone on long enough? They just stared at me like they didn't know who I was or what I was talking about.

DAY THREE
My patience snapped and I sat this one out. Ed and Didier were really into it by now, which disturbed me. I stayed in my bedroom and listened to a compilation of eighties hits that Stella had left behind; I hate that kind of music, but it was a good mundane hate and seemed to ground me a little. The others didn't even notice I wasn't with them.

DAY SEVEN
Now, they said, they were ready to begin. I sat in the garden and got drunk on my own; every time I drained a beer, I bounced the can off the Golem's vacant head.

DAY NINE
Boredom and loneliness drew me back into the front room. I'd been avoiding it since Captain's Log: Day Four, when they'd taken

to sleeping in there. The smell and the slumminess were unbelievable, and I've got quite a high squalor threshold; food, rubbish, God knows what, jumbled everywhere; a reek of vomit and faeces from two buckets in a corner; but no trace of drinking or drugs. I'd expected to open the door on a tidal wave of dope smoke and stale wine fumes, but no – just the shut-in smell of the commodes, and bad breath and sweat and unwashed plates. I noticed the bottled water, the pile of candles – the three pallets on the floor. They looked all set for a long stay. The curtains were drawn, the television turned to the wall, all the furniture pushed to the sides of the room. That was unsettling enough, but worse was the motionless, dead-looking way they all slept. I couldn't wake any of them.

DAY TEN
They slept all day, as far as I could tell. If they got up at night, I didn't hear it.

DAY ELEVEN
By now, I was wondering who to call for help. I'd already tried all our fair-weather friends; they were happy enough to come round, drink our booze and have sex with each other in their sleeping bags when the going was good, but now they all had holidays or family problems or pressing work deadlines, a great epidemic of coincidence. At that point the police were a no-no, for various reasons; family help was unforthcoming (if they'd had healthy relationships with their families, they wouldn't have been living with me in the first place); I even phoned Stella, but she told me to go kill myself instead of just talking about it all the time.

I was stuck, then. So it was a relief when they finally emerged from that stinking room – at first. I was sitting at the kitchen table looking at a handful of 10mg Valium tablets and a beige pill one of our visitors had left behind. I had no idea what the pill was, but was in such a foul, low mood I was seriously considering taking the whole lot with some mint tea. So I did. And five minutes later, they all came into the kitchen.

My first impulse of happiness faded quickly. They were talkative and friendly, a bit dazed maybe, but seemed close to normal. With my last coherent words after greeting them, I asked if they wanted anything to eat or drink: no, they must not be

22

distracted. Distracted from what? From the cross-over: the passage through the porous zone they had mapped out after days of attuning their minds.

I noticed, then, that they were humming with a sort of quiet, suppressed elation. And that they were staring around themselves at the messy kitchen, hardly blinking, as though examining things I couldn't see. Every so often one of them would give a happy, surprised little start, as though they'd seen or been touched by some fresh wonder. It took me a while to notice how strangely they were acting because I was feeling a little elevated myself, and not in a pleasant way. "Elevated" is pitching it low – I was rooted to the chair by a horrible clash of lethargy and pounding, head-spinning energy; the two opposed forces held me in a speechless, nauseated deadlock.

I could feel my pulse and core temperature shooting up even as the blood drained from my face, but they didn't notice. Engrossed and solemnly smiling, they made their way into the garden.

As he passed by, Jerry said "now we're ready to really see."

DAY TWELVE

I have no idea how I lived through the rest of that day and night. After a few hours it began to get dark, and I found I was able to lift my hand. There was still some mint tea left in the cup and I drank what little I didn't spill or slobber down my front.

A decade later, dawn came. In all this time, they hadn't come back inside and I'd heard no sound; but then, I was mainly focused on breathing and holding down the vomit I was terrified would choke me; at several points it seemed almost as if I had to will my heart to keep beating.

The morning of the twelfth day was fairly advanced and I was feeling a little better: my autonomic nervous system had taken over again, and I could imagine being able to move properly in a few more hours. "Better" is another relative term, of course; I was unprepared and unable to do anything when they came back into the kitchen and started dragging me into the garden.

I couldn't shape the words to ask what they were doing, but I could guess anyway. They were leading me toward the Golem: they wanted me to take my turn inside it. From the scraps of talk that filtered through my panic and toxicity, I realised they'd been taking turns in the "survival suit" all night; and what they'd seen had been so glorious, they wanted me to share it. They thought they were doing me a favour.

I was dragged on boneless legs to the edge of the pit by Ed and Didier, who kept up a jubilant babble over my head about how happy I'd be to see, how illuminated... Jerry shoved his starving, twitching face into mine and said, "you're not ready, but we can help you. We can influence you with our presence – and maybe you'll be able to catch sight of the place we've been, even if it's just dim, just a glimpse for a few seconds. Now we're receptive, we can go there anytime – and come back better, come back feeling like William Blake. But only with the survival suit. If you open your eyes to it outside the suit, it could crush you. But the suit makes it safe. Don't worry – the suit makes all of it safe."

Then they bundled me into the ground and shoved me into the tunnel.

For a long time I lay there, still too weak to move. The darkness and smell of dirt woke up my numbed reflexes, though; I began screaming to be let out. The effort made me afraid I was about to have a seizure, but I started crawling backwards out of the tunnel: and one of them pushed me back in. "Not until you've seen," they said, the voice too muffled by the shell of earth to be identified.

I lay there a while longer. I could hear them drifting slowly about the garden, muttering, occasionally exclaiming. I knew I had to play along with them – if only so they'd let me out – and if I could see what they were doing, perhaps I could get away unnoticed. There was silence outside. Perhaps they'd gone back indoors; I had to know. I lurched and wriggled until I was standing, propped up by the earth wall, and looked out through the eyes of the Golem.

Outside was a blazing yellow canyon. The sky was blue and full of planets whirling and colliding and multiplying like bacteria, almost too fast to watch. The rock of the canyon suddenly became sponge-like, then gaseous, and solidified back into rock – but everything had shifted. The light, the air, froze into a latticework for a second, then shattered, and everything had shifted again; now I was on a high plateau, and the planets were boiling and rebounding in a glowing plasma far below. The sky was now a mass of dark green vapours; without emotion, I knew there was an awareness up there – then perspective shifted again with a click and the vapours were close in front of me, the huge drop from the plain somehow a horizontal space at my back. While I could see nothing in the green fog, I sensed myself assessed – but not visually, not by touch or empathy or by any reasoning I could understand. It was like being removed from myself and placed in an equation, studied and balanced as an abstraction, by something that was no more than a mathematical expression itself.

There was another click and the garden reappeared around me.

I wonder now if the intelligence was trying to communicate with me; to simplify or harmonise our different fractions, modes of thought – units of thought. I think it tried, and then it scrubbed the equation and gave up. At the time, I blubbered with relief and slid out of the shell, collapsing in a heap on the tunnel floor; then I passed out for what the police told me was roughly forty-eight hours.

I came to on the grass at the other end of the garden; one of the others had put a blanket over me. Dragging myself to my feet, I leaned on the wall and struggled for breath. It was late afternoon, a plush suburban silence over everything – except for the buzzing of flies.

Curiously, when I went to investigate I didn't pass out again. Maybe I was just too mentally exhausted for strong reactions, or maybe my time in the Golem did something to me. Either way, I looked at the remains of Ed and Didier, both of them spread across a considerable area of grass, without feeling much surprise or anything else. I suppose they just couldn't wait till the suit was available again. Or they got dragged in against their wills; maybe they couldn't control the process anymore. I can't find it in myself to care.

Jerry's eyes stared out of the Golem's sockets, through me, through the house, through everything; he didn't respond when I called out to him. He seemed happy enough so I left him there for a while, but the smell in the garden finally prompted one of the neighbours to call the police.

They questioned me, of course, but they trod carefully – while they didn't believe my explanation, there was also what happened to Jerry when they dragged him kicking and screaming out of the Golem, into the open air, like a deep-sea fish risen to the surface too soon.

Actually, that's a very misleading analogy. He was wrong, see – the atmosphere in that other place wasn't crushing, wasn't heavy – it was light, impossibly light, light as thought – not even composed of what we call matter at all.

He'd gone so high, so far, that the instant he was hauled out into the grosser world, he imploded into a mist which rained over half the town.

Now as my care-worker, I ask you: can you blame me for using all the clay in the recreation room? And would it be too much to ask to be allowed to work in the garden from time to time?

PERFECTLY REASONABLE

I'm a perfectly reasonable man.

I just get scared sometimes.

In this world, who wouldn't? Reasonable enough, surely.

So I like to take care. I like to be safe; really, properly safe, safe for certain.

What I don't like would fill a phonebook – again, not surprising given the way things are – and I especially don't like nasty surprises.

I especially don't like being almost run over on my way home from a bit of quick late-night food shopping. I think you'll agree, it's hardly one of life's pleasures; so I was a little annoyed.

Granted, it was a narrow street and not very well-lit, with a sharp corner, and I should've been paying more attention crossing the road. But I was nearly home, just juggling the shopping-bag and my key (I like to have it ready to get indoors quickly, added to which if someone tries to mug you, you can punch them in the eye with it)…

And then this car slides by, I think it's going to pass the turning so I don't pick up my pace for the next kerb or anything, and without indicating, it shoots into the street and smashes the shopping bag out of my hand. There was a nasty bruise on my left leg too, but that didn't come up till the next day – one of those really deep ones that hangs around for ages and goes through about twelve different colours.

Anyway, I fell on my backside on the pavement and the car

27

stopped.

The window rolled down and a young woman poked her head out.

I thought she was going to ask if I was alright, as you'd expect, but no: she

...just...

shouted, 'Apology accepted! Fucking idiot!'

So I shouted back, 'Try indicating for once! You see those pretty little orange lights on the side of the car? They're there to be used. Give it a go, you might like it. Bitch.'

She threw open the door and stepped out. 'What did you call me?'

She was expensively dressed and well-groomed, sleek is the word I think, with one of those petulantly attractive (but not beautiful) faces that lost the habit of looking concerned about other people a long while ago. Obviously used to always being in the right; flashy job, always deferred to, never contradicted. Too much money, too young – probably out of her tree on booze and cocaine too.

I absolutely hate people like that. Don't you? Understandable, really.

So very calmly and precisely, I said, 'I called you a bitch. Which was fairly mild, taking into account your lack of consideration nearly killed me. What you actually are is a repulsive, stupid, self-centred, worthless, deluded cunt.'

This woman actually advanced on me. Can you believe it? Almost runs me over and now she's acting the injured party. It was too dark to see her expression, but from her stance I could tell she wasn't coming over to see if I was okay. Maybe it was reaction, her shock and fear coming out as anger, or maybe she genuinely was an unpleasant person.

It didn't matter; it scared me. As I mentioned, I react to being scared very, very badly.

I stood up. I was still holding my key, and now I slipped it between my third and fourth fingers and rested the tag-end against my palm, taking care not to let her see. She was too busy glaring at me anyway.

Now, anybody would've taken exception to this, in these circumstances...

Wouldn't they? And remember, I was full of nasty adrenaline.

So when she got close enough, her mouth contorting to start yelling again, I held the key at hip height and punched it into the soft part of her inner thigh as hard as I could.

When she fell down, I kicked her in the stomach, then the head.

She vomited and I felt bad, but I didn't want her attacking me.

I went through her handbag – one of those flimsy, expensive articles – looking for a rape alarm or Mace or God knows what; I wouldn't have been surprised to find a handgun.

She moved a bit, so I kicked her again. Women are much more dangerous than men: it's a well-documented fact. Why do you think they tell the army and the SAS to always shoot the female terrorists first?

Nothing in the bag, so I tossed it into the gutter and stepped over her to look at her car.

It was a lovely car; I've always wanted a nice car, and this one – barring the minor dent in the bodywork where she'd slammed into me – was a beauty.

I got in. I thought: Now look, this woman nearly squashed you into the road in this nice, nice car – the kind you've always wanted. There's a perverse sort of irony in that, isn't there?

So what could be more reasonable – more equitable – than taking it for a quick spin?

In fact, why not just keep it?

Quid pro quo.

Looking in the rearview mirror I saw her stirring again, trying to get up.

Either she was remarkably strong – and most of these young female execs go to the gym an awful lot – or whatever illegal drugs were in her system had dulled some of the pain.

Either that, or I hadn't hit her hard enough the first time.

This made me think further: You can't really in all fairness just take this car, can you? She'll complain. It'll probably make her feel inadequate, and she'll have to use public transport like the rest of us to get to work. And inevitably, she'll involve the police.

She doesn't know I actually live in this street and those identikit things are so unreliable. (Identifit? E-fit? What are they called now?)

But nevertheless.

I do not like being made nervous. I do not like it at all, the disrupted routine, the indigestion, the bad dreams, the weeks of anxiety afterward much like my bruise; no.

I watched her in the mirror a little longer and made sure the street was still empty.

Then I got out, went over to her, and broke her neck.

I learned this from a book on self-defence, a single hard chop to the windpipe, severs the spinal cord too if you do it right.

Evidently I did; and they say book learning is no substitute for practical experience (although strictly speaking, I'd now had both).

I put her body on the floor in the back, then had an agreeably relaxing drive into the country.

HOUSE BOUND

The Journal of a Gentleman:
The woman's husband was dead; all I had to do was find her and finish it. Once she was despatched, and her body given to the things in the Fissure, my wife and I could leave the house.

We could leave, finally leave, and before we did I meant to tear up the Compact and spend a few precious seconds throwing the shreds in Scrivello's face; bound by its conditions just as we were, stuck to his post, he could do nothing to stop our escape.

But the house was growing dark and beginning to change. Soon I should be lost in its immensity – and if I didn't find the woman, the things from the Fissure would take me instead; already as the house warped and distended, it became more akin to their world, and then they could emerge.

To get down to cases: how much would you wish to be immortal?

Utterly, or merely very much indeed? Everyone fears extinction and strives in some way either to deny or defer it; I have no use for those who invest in pieties and holy futurity, nor any for those who profess themselves unafraid of the prospect. These last, more and more common in this age, are especially suspect – This is the one life we have to live, they stoutly assert, and once it's done they are no longer present to be aware of its loss: if they cannot perceive it, they cannot fear that loss. Why should they wish to avoid this natural process and live forever, in any event? The monstrous boredom, the loneliness, the desolation of washing up on the rocks of another age – etcetera. Cant and shite.

If you could live forever – or, suppose, for a greatly-increased span that would *feel* like forever – you wouldn't hesitate. Certainly not if you could retain your physical wellbeing and vitality – not even if there were conditions attached.

My wife and I didn't think twice. And here we are, through our courage and greed, on the rocks of another age and no error – and revelling in it! If only our freedom of movement were less circumscribed, we'd revel still more: an orgy of expression and gratification!

We signed the Compact in – I forget the year, but shortly after Good Queen Vic's overdue death. We were both still relatively young and lusty, but neither of us quite at youth's apex any longer – rather declining toward its opposite slope with ever-greater speed. Now, of course, childishness and conceit can be extended almost indefinitely; but then, the idea was without context or referents – I blush to recall our naivety, but the current ideal of unbridled self-indulgence for a lifetime was incomprehensible. So the prospect, still dimly apprehended but growing clearer, of curtailing our pleasures and assuming that hypocritical stolidity known as *respectability*, of becoming *quaint*, was a galling one.

And so, when we met Scrivello we signed the Compact very willingly.

We met him as follows: we were the members of a small but vital and intriguing social circle, one which met in private at my old school chum Edgeworthy's place in Surrey. There, we spent many delightful weekends in stimulating conversation – elevated badinage and fabulation – and the most inventive games. Once the liquors and intoxicant sweetmeats had been thoroughly plundered, all constraint – indeed, all clothing – was cast aside and a free-for-all of Rabelasian good humour ensued.

Indeed, it was at just such a gathering that my wife and I also met; she was then a spirited ingénue from the provinces, and I marked her as a promising baggage from the first. Drawn by her bright laughter, it wasn't long before we were *intime* on the piano stool, exchanging the crudest and most direct of endearments. As I suspected, her artless façade concealed a being rich in sensuality;

and impudence, and ruthlessness – a most attractive trait, especially when one can reduce it to panting idiocy with a few well-aimed thrusts. I well remember that first night – we rode each other until her silky limbs and tresses were a-drip with the wonderful musky perspiration of roused womanhood; here was a true-bred bitch unafraid of feeding her animal nature. I was flayed raw down below for days after. Ah, we were insatiable.

Many more such nights followed, and our couplings and modes of thought proved so congruent that we cemented the bond in the accepted fashion. Not that this stopped us seeking other partners in pleasure, either together or apart; and as is the way of these things, our urge toward novelty and sensation became ever more extreme. Luckily, no-one greatly cared when a few trollops or soubrettes went missing – and no-one made the connection when their mutilated bodies were sometimes recovered.

Edgeworthy, the pusillanimous little snot, was by this time rather nervous at our ever-ramifying appetites; he began hinting, in his feeble manner, that Henrietta and I were wearing out our welcome at his parties (as well as the other guests – but they seemed a tame lot now). We had more or less decided after one more revel to cut him altogether – perhaps literally as well as figuratively – when we were introduced to Scrivello.

A scientist from the Continent, a distinguished physician and free-thinker, he was trumpeted as; a pallid, nerve-shattered voyeur, I estimated him more accurately. His mind was a perfect latrine, but he was himself powerless to act on his scurrilous fancies, thanks to a long-standing habituation to opiates. It was hilarious for Henrietta and I to hear him, minutely describing the febrile toils running through that great mind; and enact them all before him to the letter. He had a wonderful way with his fancies, and became quite a valued companion; we three retired from Edgeworthy's tea-parties to concentrate on our shared imaginings more fully.

Once intimately acquainted with us – although never on a footing of trust (he was wise in that, at least) – Scrivello shared something else. This was the project that had, apart from the violent collision of cocks and cunts he was debarred from, come to fixate him: his great work.

He unveiled this work by stages.

First, he revealed an interest in the then-discredited fad for spirit rapping, table turning and the like (the practice never goes away entirely, but fluctuates in favour with the public – this was during a downward trend). Then, he demonstrated that he had achieved contact by mediumistic means – mentalism, telepathy, call it what you will – not with departed spirits, but with another world. It was (is) just as materially present as our own, but exists on a different plane; nothing supernatural in that, as he explained through an illuminating lecture with diagrams and paraphernalia. Indeed, he said the breakthrough came to him at the close of an unusually prolonged and intense carnal reverie, one he maintained without cease for almost twenty-four hours; deprived of a physical means of expression for these images, his mind issued forth instead of his jism – this, at any rate, is his explanation. Once released, his discarnate intelligence found these beings in their sphere adjacent to ours; watching us with some curiosity, but unable till then to contact us.

He found the house after some years of looking it out – the house of the Fissure. How he detected it, and how he weakened the Fissure with assistance from those beings he'd encountered at its far point, he didn't trouble to explain. Once made, the Fissure enabled the beings to pass through – provided they had made certain adjustments to our environment without which they could not survive. The process was a temporary one and could only be repeated at lengthy intervals. It also required the expenditure of a human life; the creatures would be in need of sustenance after the journey from their world, and the effort of moulding the house to approximate its conditions. Human meat was especially toothsome to them. Ultimately, they hoped – still hope – to establish a permanent outpost in our world, but the erosion of the Fissure and adaptation of the environment are both very gradual, laborious works. To extend the environmental change beyond the house and stabilise it will... would... take an unimaginable span of time.

Luckily for them, they live forever.

Unluckily for their confederate, that's an awful lot of people to eat.

I'm sure you can see where this is all tending.

Time shortens, so I'll condense further: these creatures are of an infinitely higher material and intellectual organisation than ours, despite their savagery (or perhaps because of it – now there's a curiously satisfying thought!). They have it in their power to offer immortality to those that would help them; having found this one tiny point of entrenchment in our world, they naturally wished to pay handsomely anyone helping them to expand it.

The incentive was life eternal; the drawback was that much of it had to be spent in working for them – which is reasonable enough, when you think about it. However, it made for a form of indentured servitude; or of house-arrest, at least.

Scrivello would strive to shore up and accelerate the incursion; we would keep him company and amuse him (and them). In return, we had forever in which to amuse ourselves by rutting and gorging. All of us would be unable to leave the house for more than a few hours at any instance, and never together.

The Compact which bound us to this arrangement was, although only a piece of paper, very binding indeed; as Scrivello explained, the paper was merely a physical manifestation of a far more powerful and abstracted mechanism keeping us in our places. Whatever that meant, the creatures set great store by their stipulations and technicalities; many bodily fluids were spilled and exchanged to solemnise the deal (it reminded me of my wedding night, in fact).

Any attempt to violate the terms of the Compact would lead to an agonising death – at first a few griping pains, but the longer one stayed away from the house or declined to feed or entertain our patrons, the worse the pain would become, up to and including physical dissolution.

In Scrivello's case, he literally never felt any compulsion to leave the house. Eccentric he was, and eccentric he has remained – grown more so, naturally. So he happily stayed put, mostly out of sight on the top floor. With the advent of the internet and Viagra, I believe he spends much of his time wanking himself into a stupor; the poor fellow's hopelessly locked in his own mind and doesn't miss the real world one whit.

But as for my wife and I! My God, the frustration!

It was bad enough sitting out the Blitz, waiting to be annihilated (although we enjoyed ourselves with anyone foolish enough to wander into the house in the blackout…) – it was tolerable during the hysterically straitened years that followed (how we laughed at the scrimping, servile nation we saw going about its joyless drudgery – stoking the resentment and hatred of its children!)... It was dispiriting when those children matured and set about sating their material and sexual urges under the sanctimonious whitewash of "Free Love", and we could only look on, able to go briefly into the world in search of prey but never together, never able truly to wallow in the dirt of history... (Although again, we made the best of it – at one point the house doubled as a "commune" and we had a fine time, Henrietta and I, grinding each other in the sub-basement while the garishly-dressed juveniles suffered exquisite tortures around us; those silly drugs opened their minds to cruel manipulations by the creatures of the Fissure, hellish visitations, and we matched our hoarse pleasure to their screams of fear... Actually, damn it, it wasn't so dull after all.)

Through all the years that followed we tended our investments and sold our antiques, as all that exhilarating hatred, all those muddy undercurrents, seethed through the land – the insurrections and diseases, the wonderfully heavy-handed depredations of the State – oh, how I'd have loved to be a part of all that; with my acumen and fund of knowledge I could raise a political faction that would rule forever – and perhaps I still shall. Out of the present chaos, the clash of unreflecting Reason and unyielding irrationality, a new order must emerge... Oh, the adorable and enduring puerility of Mankind!

Through all of this, your mother and I sat on the sidelines and held the towels, as it were.

(Yes, your mother – I'd been meaning to tell you about that eventually, but could never find it in myself to be concerned overmuch; it's a little late, but now you know. It amused us to treat you as a stranger who merely happened to live in the same house, under the same limitations as us, you understand. In actual fact, you are not covered by the Compact and could have left at any time. Oh, how we roared with laughter! I wish I could see your face as you read this, my dear girl. In case you're interested, there *were* siblings over the years – none of them survived, I'm afraid.)

But now things speed toward their end.

A few months ago, Scrivello told us that a great advance had been made; the creatures of the Fissure had bent their great wills and minds to speeding up the incursion, and had devised a way of breaking through in one great spasm. They would need Scrivello to oversee and direct their energies at this end; they would need us to keep them well-fuelled. In other words, we either fed them, or got fed to them – at the critical moment, it wouldn't matter who was hurled in to be consumed. They would pour from the Fissure and, in the scant minutes when the bridge-head hung in flux between permanence and collapse, they would devour anyone they found who wasn't a snivelling little foreign turd of a scientist.

High stakes, indeed. And it was work enough feeding them in the period leading to this final effort. How were we to attract enough people to satisfy them?

Simplicity itself – we advertised the house for sale.

It's always been the same – most house-hunters are simply looking without intent to purchase as a way to fill empty lives, bereft of friends to notice their disappearance; and nobody ever misses an estate agent.

The final day began inauspiciously:

'Wake up, you lout. The walls have changed again,' said Henrietta.

Now, you've never been allowed into our boudoir, have you? Quite right, too. It's similar to what the more affluent sucklings of this era have; all modern conveniences, as you might be aware (you ought to be – you went out and purchased them on our behalf, as well as all the other skivvying you've done over the years, darling girl).

In any case, had you ever seen our room and lived, you would have noticed at once that something was amiss.

The walls, ordinarily gleaming white, had turned dark blue overnight. A not-unpleasing shade, veined with streaks of lighter blue that fluoresced gently and threw strange purple shadows.

'So I see,' I replied with commendable patience. 'How are we to show off the house when it's in metamorphosis?'

With equal patience, she said, 'My own sweet oaf, it doesn't matter. They'll be dead before they see anything they oughtn't.'

She slipped from the bed and examined her nude form in the glass, scanning it for imperfections and of course finding none; held suspended in the prime of life, she remained utterly captivating. I looked away – hard as it may be to credit, we had reached an odd stage in our sensual existence; we had passed beyond gross carnality, to a state of the sternest chastity (all the

37

better to start again from the beginning, you see). In this frame of mind, the most erotic thing of which I can conceive is *not* to sustain an erection; but sadly this is beyond me. Before the inevitable could occur and distract me, I too got up and dressed hastily. We had a viewing in two hours' time.

The couple who came to see the house seemed pleasant enough; it was clear at a glance they'd be easy to kill.

The heifer was a small, nervous woman with protuberant eyes; her bullock an equally meagre specimen, with poor posture and overly-youthful clothes. I cannot abide the current vogue for abstract facial hair, especially among the middle-aged, and made a mental note to dispose of him first.

We ushered them into the hallway. 'It's much larger than I expected,' said the woman, in a daunted but greedy tone. 'Usually those websites make the pictures, you know, make everything look bigger,' she carried on, her companion nodding ingratiation.

'Yes, well, we do rattle around in here rather,' I said, shepherding them into the dining room. I was on the look-out for any further signs of spatial disturbance from the Fissure, but spotted none as yet. 'Of course, the top floor's occupied by our landlord.'

Both frowned. 'Landlord? Hang on, I thought –' the man said.

I'd spoken distractedly as I glanced around the room to be sure all was normal; Henrietta shot me a warning look. 'A figure of speech only,' I said.

'What Edmund means is, the man who sold us this house now lives in the garret,' said my wife. 'But he'll be gone too.'

'Fine, Henrietta – it is Henrietta, isn't it?' said the man. Insufferable familiarity!

'Yes. You may call me Mrs Byrely.'

There was a moment's awkward silence, then we led them into the parlour. The walls here were thick, and easily cleaned after each viewing – as was the carpet (some modern fabric that doesn't stain). Not that that would matter soon; but we couldn't have them bolting at the sight of old blood.

(page missing – next entry barely-legible, written in haste)
'It needs blood,' Henrietta said through clenched teeth, 'to work

properly.' She was crowding him up to the slab and breathing heavily in his ear; his jugular jumped with fright as she bored the knife-point against, then into it. He screamed and a mist of blood beaded the blue stones, which began to moan and extrude teeth.

Somewhere impossibly far away, *deep* away, began a faint unbroken whispering.

'Now find that woman!' Henrietta shouted – positively screamed – at me. Now I ask you, however was I to know such a broken-down old jade could run so fast? Well, much good it did her – though not for the expected reason, daughter mine. You deceitful little slut.

(page stained)

(journal continued in different handwriting)
Oh, my parents. You never fooled me, you know. I was always only too aware I had your foul genes. I'm the daughter you never had; except you *did*. Authors of my misery, and a pair who truly deserved each other. And deserved me – I'm only a little further up the spiritual and evolutionary ladder, after all; how could it be otherwise?

Foisting this vile book on me with a jibe and a smirk was merely the final wound in a lifetime of insults. And I paid you back in full. Boorish, grasping, ludicrously ego-ridden – you were easy enough to fool, sodden with your own coarseness and selfish "pleasures" – utterly incapable of introspection (or of observing others – like me, for instance – observing you)... and not a shred of original thought (or sin) between you. A father capable of planning any foulness and a mother still more capable of expediting it: vain, play-acting bitch, how you enjoyed seeing yourself as an edged and deadly-accurate weapon, speeding on some death-errand for your uncouth husband.

As we skulked in this big, decrepit house and I did my best to ignore your predilections – not always easy when I could be dragged into it all on a whim, either through threat, coercion or literal brute force... As we skulked – I plotted to kill you. The only reason I endured it was to find a way, to wait out my chance to destroy this family root and branch. Then burn down the house and salt the earth, and curse it. I read your (huge, wasteful and neglected) library of history: those Romans knew a few things about bearing a grudge.

39

So first of all, I killed the woman myself, before you could get to her: and spoiled her in a way that left her quite unfit as an offering. Then I found Scrivello, cowering at his desk... The sight of me touching my naked body was enough to give him convulsions. As he thrashed, he cracked his skull open on a paperweight. It was an easy matter after that to use some of his alchemical notes as spills, lit at the open fire, and start feeding your house to the flames. I'm writing this by the lovely glow of the curtains burning, and if I'm lucky you'll find it in your futile efforts to escape. I won't know for sure, because being immune, unbound by that stupid Compact, *I* can leave whenever I like. Not that I care what happens to me next – I just wanted you to know who engineered this; and you'll probably need some reading matter where you're going.

I wonder what punishment your patrons from elsewhere will see fit to visit on you...?

(journal ends)

It was the third week of his rehabilition, and he was getting nervous. They'd been so very very good to him so far – hadn't they? Whoever they were, they were kind: they'd told him so. And they fed him and housed him and kept him. But somewhere around the sixteenth day, a malaise of anxiety and inertia began to settle over him. There was little to do, and little to read – just one book, an old one, handwritten. It meant nothing to him; it was gibberish. He slept badly, spent hours pacing his spherical living-quarters, sitting down and jolting up again, staring through the window. It was a black porthole painted onto one of the walls, a representation only, but looking at it calmed him – he could almost imagine it was real, the permanent night it symbolized, the one he lived inside. And he could almost see eddies and veils of shadow, huge shapes, moving beyond it. Looking at the gleaming black window-picture, he tried to keep faith – but it was hard to imagine ever being let out into the darkness it signified. They'd told him that when he was ready, they would allow this – then there would be games. During that day's feeding, he found he had little appetite for the nutrient gel pumped in through the wall. He submitted to the feeding-tube with ill grace, almost with disgust. The tube retracted into the wall with a slithery smack, leaving a small pool of gel, grey and lukewarm, on the floor – the floor that his eyes could never quite focus on, that seemed to vibrate. Perhaps, he thought, my feeding-palp is underdeveloped. There was no-one to ask; he folded himself into his cot and tried to sleep as the lights flickered down to purple.

On the twentieth day, he was very worried. Externally, the process of transformation advanced, but internally he felt something close to panic — and the ever-present inertia too. His instinct was paralysed between the two opposing feelings; he didn't know what to do, or even if anything should be done. Should he call in the nurse? He'd never seen her, but they told him he'd once known her well. She must be much more advanced than he, to have attained such a responsible position already. No, he couldn't call on her, he thought as he lay staring up at the floating purple light. He couldn't trouble her over something so trivial.

Somewhere early into the next day, the question became academic. The nurse called on him; and her treatments, despite everything he'd been told, were not kind at all.

THE NICOTINE CENTRE

It sounded too good to be true – but so what if it was? He was desperate to believe it. The treatment was free, the place looked nice and the people seemed fine. What could it hurt?

If he could quit – finally quit – the potential benefits were so great he couldn't bring himself to calculate them. Benefits to everything; health, self-esteem, the sketchy situation with Judy (his inability to save money or muster the wind for sex anymore, frankly). Fake or not, quackery or homeopathic nonsense or whatever, it just had to be tried; foolishness any other way.

So, Burton signed the release form at the front desk and let them lead him to his room.

It was a lovely room, modern and comfortable, with expensive bed linen and towels and shower products, and a plush bathrobe monogrammed with the Nicotine Centre logo. This was a more elegant, art deco version of the standard "no smoking" symbol, but picked out in fine gold thread and with a faint suggestion of night sky and stars behind: freedom, expanded possibilities.

'Classy,' said Burton, and settled on the bed to wait to be called for his first consultation.

The phone on the dresser buzzed, and he was asked to go see Doctor Prince on the third floor.

'Mister Burton. May I call you Theodore? Ted?'

'Ted's fine, ta. Never could get on with Theodore – too much to live up to. I blame the parents.' Burton forced a jolly laugh that didn't quite come off; that could be the itch in his throat, the one that by now he'd have deadened with a cigarette.

Doctor Prince was a well-groomed, ageless man with a pleasingly genuine smile; he was really looking at Ted, studying him, and leant forward over the desk in a listening pose. 'We'll get to what's behind your habit in due course; the sources of anxiety that make it a compulsion. But the main thing is simply to get you off the ciggies, starting from now. When did you last have a smoke?'

'When I got out of the taxi just before I booked in,' said Burton with a shrug. 'Seemed a good idea at the time.'

'I'm sure it did. And in the short term, from your point of view it was, strange as that sounds. Still, if it's any comfort I think we can start to help you right away.'

Burton looked out through the window past the Doctor's sympathetic face for a moment, allowing his eyes to take in the large house and grounds, the hillsides pleated with trees, the far-off train station. God, this place was idyllic. And this room – it even *smelt* expensive, all pale cream and deep leather chairs. 'You know, I think my sense of smell's already started coming back,' said Burton. His voice sounded strange to him; half pleased, surprised even, and half stalling for time: time for one more cigarette before they began.

Doctor Prince nodded his understanding. 'We see this a lot. Your senses seem heightened because this is a very stressful situation for you – that's all it is, a psychosomatic stress reaction. But come with me and we'll see if we can't relax you a little.'

They stood, and Burton followed him out.

'How?' he said rather more loudly than he'd meant to; people glanced round in the pastel corridor as they walked past elevators and potted plants, abstract prints on the walls. Something else was bothering him too, but he couldn't isolate it now; his palms were sweating, his chest and scalp felt too tight.

Doctor Prince chuckled, not unkindly. 'A mild herbal relaxant. No needles or anything, promise.'

'You'll be with me all the time?' Now they were descending a short flight of marble steps.

'For the introductory examination. We need to assess the level of initial treatment – and then, if you'll pardon the corny sentiment, you can begin to be free.'

Free. That was it: that was what was bugging him. 'Doctor...?'

They were approaching a green baize door like something from a Victorian gentlemen's club. Doctor Prince raised an eyebrow as he held the door open for Burton. 'Please be assured, any last-minute nerves are totally unwarranted.'

'No, it's more... Well, not something bothering me exactly, really appreciate all this, but... am... a bit puzzled.'

Doctor Prince gave a shrewd twinkle. 'Why would we go to all this trouble, perhaps? And at no charge?'

'Exactly. It wasn't quite clear when you got in touch, I read your... uh, circular really carefully, and your emails, but they didn't seem to say. Don't think I'm trying to ask, you know, What's in it for you or anything, but I just thought – how do you manage all this? It must be incredibly expensive.'

'The old, sweet story: a consortium of rich benefactors.'

They were still hovering in the doorway but Doctor Prince showed no sign of impatience.

Burton could see a wood-panelled passage, gleaming with polish and concealed lighting, another expensive meld of old and new. 'Anyone I've heard of?'

'Ah, no. They're very private.'

'And why me? I don't even know how you chose me – it was like winning the lottery.'

'In a sense, that's what you've done. Come with me, please.'

The baize door sealed behind them, enclosing them in the pleasantly chilly, scrubbed atmosphere of the hallway. 'I'm very grateful. Never mind all this posh stuff and VIP treatment – not that I object – but the Vogler-Lynch Treatment looks quite pricey, all the research and that.'

Doctor Prince frowned for a moment. 'Of course, you looked it up on the internet.'

'Didn't I just. Sounds wonderful, but expensive: like rehab,' and Burton attempted another laugh. 'Because it's so new, I suppose.'

'Yes,' said Doctor Prince, leading the way so that his face was hidden. 'Because it's new.'

'I couldn't get much info on it, actually – what it involves. Oh, nothing bad: everyone said it really worked, all great publicity. But not much detail.'

'Trade secrets of the consortium. And you, Ted, are about to

44

be let in on those secrets. In here, if you would.'

They stepped into an empty room.

There was no carpet, no furniture, and plaster sagged from the walls. By the light from a small, grimy window close to the water-stained ceiling, Burton saw cobwebs and dust, a disused fireplace.

There was a splintery click as Doctor Prince locked the door. 'We can begin,' he called out to someone else beyond Burton.

Stumbling to look, Burton saw a second door in the opposite wall.

It opened stiffly, half off its hinges, and a woman in white plastic overalls and a hairnet came in. She was holding a black box in one gloved hand, the size and shape of something a ring or necklace might be kept in.

Suddenly Burton needed to release a hacking smoker's cough, but held it down with an effort of will that nearly collapsed his legs. 'What is this?'

'This,' said Doctor Prince, gesturing to the woman, 'is one of our benefactors.'

'So can't she – won't she tell me what's going on?'

Prince shook his head, still smiling that amiable collegiate smile. 'Not her. That's Ms Hickey. I mean this.'

Burton realised Prince was pointing at the box just as the woman began to slowly, carefully prise it open.

There was something moving inside.

'How's it going, mate? Feel any better yet?'

Burton smiled at the man on the bench beside him, reflecting that in any other place they'd probably both be smoking, asking each other for a light, all that sad stuff. He looked out over the grounds and drew a deep near-autumn breath. 'Much, cheers. You too, I'm guessing.'

'Lordy yes. Haven't had a single puff in...' his eyes wandered vaguely, '...Must be nearly three weeks. It's brilliant.'

'That long, eh.' A pause. 'Me too. Got any idea how long they're planning on keeping us here, now I come to think of it? I've had a lovely time and all, but...'

The man pursed his lips. 'Can't remember offhand. Still, lovely grub, scenery... I'm not complaining.' He was older than Burton and thinner, unshaven, with an underslept look and unwashed blondish hair; his eyes darted about and his hands had a

45

minute tremor.

And, Burton suddenly realised, he smelt strongly of cigarette smoke.

Something made Burton look down at his own hands, resting on his knees.

They were shaking too, the index and middle fingers stained yellow with nicotine.

The only reason he hadn't noticed the smell of tobacco on the man sooner was because he reeked of it himself.

Everything seemed to brighten and dull simultaneously: *Why – how – hadn't he noticed this long before?*

'Back in a minute,' he said, getting up. His temples were throbbing and he could barely speak above a whisper.

The man nodded vaguely, and glancing back Burton half-expected to see him lighting a cigarette; but he was just staring at his fidgeting hands.

'I'd like to see Doctor Prince, please,' he said at the front desk.

The girl's bland smile as she keyed in Prince's number told him No, so he reached for the most provocative thing he could think of – he searched his pockets for cigarettes. He couldn't find any.

'Never mind,' he said. 'Think I'll just go for a lie down. Not feeling too good.' Burton hurried for the elevator without caring whether he'd convinced her or not.

He was surprised that he reached Doctor Prince's office without any trouble; and when he shoved open the door without knocking, the Doctor looked up from a sheaf of papers with an unruffled smile.

'I want a word with you,' Burton panted. His chest felt hammered – felt, in fact, like he'd been smoking forty a day.

'I take it you're unhappy with your Treatment.'

'Too bloody right. I want an explanation and no hassle. I want to speak to whoever's in charge here for once.'

'As I explained before, the consortium prefer a hands-off approach.'

'Tough. You get one of them down here or on the phone right now or I'm walking. And when I do, I'm going to the police, the papers –' he floundered, 'my MP, everyone.' Then another thought struck him with a cold weight of shock. 'And while you're at it, give me back my mobile. I don't remember saying you could take it off me.'

Doctor Prince shook his head, palms up. 'You're determined, aren't you. Okay.'

He reached into his desk.

The small black box was unfamiliar but Burton staggered, almost folding at the middle, under the flood of revulsion the sight of it threw over him.

'Here's our chief fundraiser,' said Doctor Prince.

The box clicked open and a scrabbling, restless noise echoed from it, somehow far too distant and large for such a small container.

Burton groped for the door.

There was a clicking and slobbering, then a mass of tangled, colourless fibres exploded out of the box, mushrooming into the air and growing as it flowed outward.

It flopped onto the carpet, then with a horribly muscular leap attached itself to Burton's leg.

The room was vast and metal-walled, and thick with cigarette smoke.

Burton could make out little detail from where he lay clamped to a shelf, partly due to the clouds of smoke but mostly because he was unable to move.

All around, the room echoed with coughing and retching, the gasps of exhausted smokers.

Doctor Prince leaned over him, wafting away some of the fumes. 'I hope you're satisfied,' he said, voice still mild and amused.

'What... was that stuff in your office –' Burton strained his head against whatever glued it to the ledge, but couldn't see or feel his legs. 'Is it still on me?'

'No, it's got far more important things to do. It just secreted a neural inhibitor enzyme, the usual sort of thing.'

'The usual sort of thing – your herbal relaxant.' Perhaps Burton was getting high on all the smoke; it was an effort to think or feel clearly; seeing Doctor Prince's compassionate but disinterested smile, he embraced this lack of affect. The fear would be much worse.

'Of course. Who do you think's been treating you every night?

The Treatment's not a human invention, don't be so silly; even if we could devise something that effective, you think the tobacco lobby would allow it, or all those lovely charities who get their funding from anti-smoking propaganda, all of them tied together like symbiotes?'

Burton didn't want to make the connection, but couldn't stop himself. 'Symbiotes.'

'Yes. Our backers implant a small strand of tissue into your neck, so there's no danger of rejection when the Treatment begins. Over time, it matures enough to relay signals from you to the rest of the Group.'

'Signals.'

'Pleasure impulses, Ted. They *love* their cigarettes, but they're even more prone to unpleasant side-effects than we are. Don't ask me how they got hooked – it's a long story. They travel a lot, pick up local habits.'

'So we're...'

'Smoking for them, yes. Once the connections have been made, it's like a mainline to constant bliss, tickling away – it must be lovely for them.'

'But what's in it for us? Symbiosis, you said.'

'Well, they can remove unpleasant memories. They can reverse or delay some of the worst aspects of smoking for you, if you want to continue on this basis (everyone figures out the deal sooner or later). And in the long run, they could be of great help to the human race: they're so grateful already. No poison weeds where they're from; it's horribly dull there in general, I'm told.'

A gag reflex was struggling vaguely in his oesophagus, but Burton felt too mellowed on nicotine to follow through; it subsided, but not his unease. 'I've got an alien body inside me.'

'And have had for some time. Just like everyone else in this room, including me. It's not so bad really, is it? Think of it as a living nicotine patch.'

Burton tried to focus. 'I still feel awful, though. Really awful, like when I was smoking heavily. And I can't even lift my head.'

'That's because the node on the back of your neck's extruding itself to feed the main Group.'

This time, Burton did gag. He even found it in himself to writhe on the ledge.

Prince pulled a wry face. 'I wouldn't. They can get very

irritable if the feeding's disrupted; just stay still and you'll get some nice sleepy enzymes before too long.'

The harsh barks of the unseen smokers dinned off the walls.

'You're lying. You're lying about all this. It's something else – I'm not even smoking right now.'

Doctor Prince glanced at his watch. 'Digested version: yes. I'm lying. There's nothing you can do about it, though; you shouldn't barge into people's offices like that. Now that I'm sure you can't cause a nuisance, I needn't lie any more; besides, I've work to do.' He began to move out of Burton's line of sight. 'Digested version – I like that. Very apt. Nicotine is their vice, but they have to eat too you know.'

Burton lay still, as he could do nothing else, and realised he did have some sensation left after all; he could feel something cold and dry start to crawl on his neck.

He closed his eyes as it slipped around and touched his cheek, then began to explore his face.

BITTEN BY THE BIRDS OF PARADISE

'Hideous, aren't they. They don't look real.'

'What's wrong with them?'

'You know that book… The French bloke who goes all decadent and mental?'

'Er.' She smiled with a frown. 'That covers a lot of the stuff you read.'

Tony stared off across the botanical gardens at the sea, pretending thought; actually he was just inhaling the warm liquid compound of salt air, sunlight and massed unfamiliar scents. Christmas abroad: so much smarter, a more civilised treat than England in the perma-dusk, trapped with the family. 'You know – he only likes plants that look artificial, unreal sensations, playing a piano that shoots out absinthe and wanking – Huysmans wrote it… Christ, what's it called again?'

'*Against Nature.*' Ellen sharpened her smile into the playful nip of sarcasm they both enjoyed. 'You need to stop boozing so much. Your memory's starting to go.'

They both knew he remembered author and title really, was liking the role of fuddled Brit abroad.

'I can't help it if they make such nice wine here. Tastes like mince pies and Xmas pud, but better. And yes, that was it – *Against Nature*. And I am. Against it, if it looks like those horrible fucking things.'

He pointed at the group of flowers they'd paused beside.

They were gaudy and metallic-looking, with swan-necked

stems curving into crests – quills, even – of dagger-like petals in bright, almost fluorescent colours. These were fixed to a thicker out-growth of nude vegetable head that looked unpleasantly bony and avian. The effect was exactly that of some malign toy, a robot/bird hybrid designed to scare children.

'I think they're quite nice.'

'Yeah, but you're one far-out freaky chick, man.'

'You need to stop reading those crappy seventies sci-fi novels, too. It's infecting your speech, and besides all those "chicks" in leather on the covers with long hair and big tits make me feel inadequate.'

'Ah, go scrub the kitchen floor.'

She punched him lightly on the arm. They were still standing on the crazy-paved path between the trees, staring side by side at the flowers.

'Speaking of sci-fi...' Tony leaned closer to the flowers with a grimace of distaste, wondering if they smelt as wrong as they looked, trying to find a placard or name-tag. 'I'm thinking John Wyndham now. Imagine these fuckers getting up and coming after you. They've got beaks. Sharp ones.'

'They're birds of paradise.'

He straightened and stared at her, arming a light sweat from his forehead. 'Seriously? Is that their actual name or are you just spinning a beautiful lacework of words?'

'That's their actual name, arsehole.'

'How did you know that?'

'It's in the guidebook, if you could be bothered to read it. The island's famous for them – biggest, most varieties, that sort of thing.'

'I thought it was onions.'

'Well, onions and those.'

'Euuchh. I'd keep it quiet if I was the tourist board. Look, they're – those colours, they're so tarty. Like someone's sprayed them with make-up.'

'That doesn't entirely make sense, dear.'

'You know what I mean. They're like a prozzie who'd threaten you with a dirty needle. Let's get away from them and get back in the shade, please. Indoor shade with cool drinks.'

'Alkie.' She looked tempted, though.

'It's Christmas. Besides, they're so damn polite and proper

here, it's a pleasure to hand over your money. Just think: we could be in a Wetherspoons right now eating lukewarm turkey slabs with your mum.'

'Or sitting in complete silence watching Victoria Wood with yours.'

They walked away down the winding path, between sinuous branches and fronds, toward the hotel bar that looked down on the tide meeting the rocks.

That night, Tony had an awful dream.

The birds of paradise had indeed begun to move, flocking after him in the dark. They called out to him in discordant, tinkling voices that promised pleasures unthinkable, if only he'd stop and let them peck at him with their sweetly-venomed beaks. They stumbled slowly, clumsy and flightless, but he knew they wouldn't ever stop; from the blackness all around came a crumbling whisper of dry soil as more of them uprooted themselves to pursue him.

Where was he? It wasn't the botanical garden at the hotel. It was a huge, ill-defined tangle of root and branch, humid and rugged, cratered, blind – and behind him, the patter of rubbery, vegetable feet.

And their voices…

We love you Tony
Come with us Tony
We'll bite you Tony
It feels so good Tony
Happy screams Tony
Murder and quiver Tony
Childish dead realms Tony
Come with us Tony
Show you clouds bleed Tony
Eyeless fire-orgy Tony
We'll bless you Tony
Saintly and sweet Tony
Brute numbness Tony
We love you Tony

…He stumbled and screamed as they overwhelmed him in a passionless scramble.

The next day wasn't so good.

Tony sat on the balcony of their room until evening, barely moving, barely speaking to Ellen; he felt bad about that, but the dream – or something else, let it be something else, some winter bug picked up at home, anything – had wrung him out. He watched as night returned, steeling himself with the local brandy; eventually, he couldn't have moved or spoken if he'd wanted to. Ellen tried hard to engage him, to draw him out; eventually her face hardened and she retreated into the bedroom.

He watched the creamy waves, the orderly tiers and cubes of light in the hills; clean and silent, an odd blend of cultivation and bleakness with some elusive underlying logic. He tried to find it; read the striated landscape for clues.

Cultivation… Everywhere he looked, he saw patches of those awful flowers.

He dreamt he was pursued again.

Back in the hell-scape, the airless, lightless wilderness, staggering over rocks and bones. Behind him, the massing flocks of flower-birds, their chase mechanical and relentless; they sang to him in a brittle, piping choir.

He was overwhelmed again.

…And woke up sprawled in the chair out on the balcony under a grey sky, the hiss of sea and foliage loud in his ears.

'Jesus,' he choked out, reaching for and knocking over the near-empty bottle.

As he leaned down, something hopped over the parapet and pecked him on the hand.

Ellen woke up to find Tony's side of the bed empty.

Another sunny day strained through the blinds; either he'd passed out on the balcony or slipped into bed without her noticing, was now in the bathroom with head in hands, trying to squeeze out the hangover.

Either way, he'd be fine… Wouldn't he?

Cursing herself for being passive, for enabling, she got up and went to look for him.

Tony stood naked in the bathroom, gazing at himself in the mirror. He was pale and glassy-eyed, and smiling in a way she'd never seen before and didn't like. His eyes switched to meet hers in the glass at his shoulder.

'You okay?' she said.

'Oh, yes.' His voice was quiet and toneless.

'Of course you are, you lucky slob. You passed out outside, didn't you? Imagine if that'd happened at home. You'd have frozen to death.' Really she was just making sounds, trying to elicit a normal response, get rid of this smirking stranger and speak to Tony again.

'I'm very well,' he said in the same neutral, stoned-sounding way.

'Have you been – are you on something, did you take something last night?'

He looked puzzled for a moment – began to nod, then shook his head. Shrugged. Smirked more widely and said, '"Beware, beware his flashing eyes and floating..." You know the poem, right?'

She folded her arms and took a step back, scowling and not wanting to; unable to prevent herself. 'What's wrong with you? Are you ill or what?'

'No. I'm a bird with crystal plumage. I'm a phoenix – or possibly a swan.'

They had a game, a private joke, whereby they'd work the titles and characters from as many old horror films into conversation with others as possible; in this situation, coming from this strange new version of her best and closest friend, it tightened her nerves painfully. 'Oh for fuck's sake. Not now, Tony. Just tell me what's the matter. Please.'

'Nothing. Everything's sublime. I feel really... pre-Christian.'

'You're starting to scare me. Stop it.'

'There's no need to be scared. I was scared of them, but they're not really the way they seem. They want to help us feel good. Look.' He pointed at the glass.

'It's a mirror. Okay, and...?' Humour him, she thought, humour him and make it go away, or get him settled down and get help. But just humour him.

'Can't you see them? They're with us now. I've joined the flock.'

'Tony,' her voice cracked, scalded, 'what are you talking about?'

54

'Look in the mirror and tell me what you see.'

'I see...' Her eyes caught and held his. Then there was a flicker, and what she saw made her scream – if only briefly.

They found him in the botanical gardens once the hotel management called them in. Calm, wary, dark-eyed people in uniform, they approached the Englishman slowly and carefully.

He was sitting in the middle of a crushed mass of flowers – birds of paradise – and singing to himself. He was smiling. Every so often, he would stroke the plants he was enmeshed in; once, he seized one and took a bite out of its brilliant-petalled head, chewing till green juice covered his chin. Beside him lay his girlfriend, staring sightlessly up at the sky in a congealing sheet of blood. She was covered in stab-wounds – they were tiny, possibly made by nail-scissors, a corkscrew, some other small implement; and they resembled the marks of many beaks.

DEATHBED

Trent wondered why the old people became more agitated after dark.

Maybe it was disorientation; sedatives wearing off, they woke in an unfamiliar bed under fluorescent half-light. They were confined in a narrow space surrounded by curtains, machines, unidentifiable noises, with tubes in their arms and sticking to their faces. Many of them weren't even aware they were in hospital, and the nurses' reassurances were forgotten minutes or even seconds later.

This was what he told himself at first; after the third hour of the second night, his patience was exhausted and so was he.

By four a.m. he thought he might be ready to commit murder again.

Trent had been admitted to the acute medical ward after going on an alcoholic binge and vomiting blood; it wasn't the first time he'd gone on a bender, but he'd had plenty of time between Librium capsules to reflect it might have to be his last.

Shaking, sweating and biting down nausea, he'd tried not to hate everyone around him and mostly succeeded.

Except after lights out.

The old bastards just wouldn't – couldn't – shut up. Of course their lives and minds were in ruins; he was forced to admit these people were a great advert for not living too long. They didn't recognize their relatives, accused anyone who passed within their erratic awareness of being impostors or thieves; they held rambling arguments with people who weren't there or cried out in misery.

God, did they cry out.

Trent thought of the doctor who'd inserted a finger into his anus the previous afternoon to check for rectal bleeding, of the endoscopy camera that'd been reeled down his throat on what felt like six feet of garden hose – every muscle in his body had clenched against the invasion. Now *those* were things to whine about, had he been so inclined.

How could the indignities of a deteriorating body compare if its tenant didn't even comprehend them – spent all day asleep and all night shouting, babbling about the Spanish Civil War?

The man in the bed next to Trent's was old, but not ancient enough to have experienced this long-ago war, yet talked of nothing else. He insisted it had started in 1973 and was still going on; books had been written about the incredible length of this war, books that had as yet no endings; as soon as they were finished the war would be over. He was very keen to know what the newest chapter said; his single-mindedness and energy were frightening.

If he didn't shut up, Trent was going to smother him with a pillow.

The old woman opposite was worse because she was mobile and aggressive. In the end, she'd become such a nuisance the nurses had tranquillized her.

Trent lay with knotted stomach and cursed his saline drip every time he tried to shift onto his side. His head ached from fatigue and the man's incessant bellowing.

Every so often a trolley would rattle past in the open corridor a few feet away, or a door would bang. Sometimes a nurse would come in and talk sense to the man in a suppressed furious hiss.

After a few seconds' quiet, he'd start up again.

It was no good – Trent had to kill him.

Slowly, he began working the drip out of the cannula in his arm. There was blood, but he caught most of it in the ball of tissues on his bedside locker; the saline he left to collect in his water glass. Then he swung out of bed and waited a moment, listening to the old man.

The man was speaking in a quieter tone, almost reasonable, as if arguing mildly with an old friend. He said, 'Please could you give to me... A drop of electricity, just a drop... So I can speak to my wife.'

57

'Yes, I can help you,' said Trent quietly, then whipped the pillow from beneath the man's head and held it over his face.

One skinny arm flailed for the alarm button, but Trent batted it away. After a surprisingly short time, the old man was dead. They'd find him in the morning, so sad, slipped away in the night – well, he was very weak after all.

Trent replaced the pillow carefully, looked round to make sure he was unobserved, then got back into bed, fumbling with the cannula till it was more or less re-connected; if questioned, he could've rolled over in his sleep and dislodged it; it wasn't leaking badly and looked convincing enough. No CCTV on this ward, no nurses around – no problem.

And now perhaps I *will* be able to get some sleep, he thought; glancing at the still form in the next bed, he sank into the coarse mattress and smiled.

Trent greyed out for a while, not fully asleep but no longer aware of his surroundings.

It had been a tough few weeks; the drinking certainly didn't help – not when it got out of hand – though up till then, it gave him the energy and focus he needed.

Hurting or killing people for a living wasn't as lucrative as books and films might make you think; you had to maintain quite a work-rate. Plus, you had to keep your edge, your taste for the job. It wouldn't do to give your employers the impression you were burning out, losing the drive: that would be very dangerous.

Still, it didn't matter to him; it wasn't as if the people he killed were particularly real anyway. He sometimes felt he alone was real; they were like lath and plaster to be torn down, torn through.

No more whiskey, though; nice expensive wines from now on, he thought, drifting off.

A hand was pinching his arm.

Must be the nurse – more pills or endless blood tests. 'Fuck off,' he mumbled, blinking in the half-light and wriggling away. Through half-open lids he could see the ward was still in semi-darkness – couldn't a man get some rest?

The hand pinched tighter, wringing the muscle viciously, and Trent was suddenly full awake.

'I said fuck –' His voice fell dead in his throat, blocking it.

The old man from the next bed had hold of his arm.

He was grinning, all his teeth bared, and his eyes glittered with black vitality. Trent knew the man was dead; he had checked his breathing and pulse.

The hand gripping Trent was very cold and strong. As Trent tried to shrink back, the old man leant forward, grin widening further, and brought his face very close. Trent could feel no breath from the gaping mouth, but the man spoke:

'Now I've got you, you Communist traitor. No more war for you, friend.'

'What do you mean?' he said in a bleating, breathless voice he'd heard before only in his nightmares.

'You're now officially my prisoner. Get up, peasant.' The man dragged him to his feet with a single jerk and began herding him out into the corridor.

His IV lines pulled over their stand with a crash, but no-one came; Trent realised there was no sound, no sense of occupancy, in the hospital around him at all.

The feeling of unreality that had insulated Trent so far began to desert him when he saw how dark and empty the corridor was.

The man shuffled Trent further into the shadows, the loose back of his gown flapping.

'Where are you taking me?'

'I still need electricity. For my wife,' said the man, and sniggered.

Trent tried to dig in his heels, but they squeaked frictionlessly over the linoleum and the dead man was too strong. 'Where are you taking me?' he said again.

Halfway along the corridor, a white-clad figure stood watching them.

Trent's voice swelled back and he made an incoherent cry for help.

The figure didn't react, and as they drew closer he saw that it was a middle-aged woman in a hospital smock. Her mouth and chin were crusted with dried blood and her eyes were glazed and cunning, like the old man's. She watched with head on one side as they passed and smiled crookedly.

'Nearly there,' said the old man.

They passed through swing doors into a small room so blindingly green under harsh light that at first Trent didn't understand what he was seeing. Once his sight had adjusted – and the man pushed him closer to the centre of the room – he still didn't understand.

Filling the room, a room he was sure hadn't been there before, was a mass of pipes and wires and cylinders. Its rusted surface was barbed with levers and dials. 'What's... What's that?' said Trent.

'The machine. To extract electricity, for my wife. The electricity you traitors have been hoarding.'

Trent began to fight. He punched, kicked, gouged, butted and elbowed – the repertoire of a lifetime. But the man pushed him effortlessly toward the machine, where a black aperture was sliding open.

As he stumbled and fell into the hole, Trent began to scream.

Someone was hammering on his bedside table.

Trent coughed and sat up.

Sunlight filled the ward; the bed beside his was empty. A large black woman was staring at him in irritation.

'Do you want your breakfast or not?' she snapped.

'Oh... God, yes.'

She wheeled the table into position and planked down a tray of cornflakes and toast. 'Tea or coffee?'

'Er, tea.'

She slopped some into a mug and moved away with her trolley.

Around him, the ward was filled with warmth and smells, some aseptic and some unpleasantly ripe, and the clatter of activity. Nurses shuttled back and forth in the corridor; he could hear traffic and wind in the trees through the open window, smell pollen.

The bed beside his was empty, definitely empty, and looked as though it always had been.

Jesus fucking Christ. I have *got* to cut down the booze, he thought.

When the nurse came with his first dose of Librium he considered asking – Was there an old man there last night? Did he die?

But that seemed somehow unwise, and besides she was preoccupied with the mess he'd made of the cannula and IV lines. He produced the shame-faced smile he'd practiced many times in front of the mirror, and she went away mollified.

Before too long, the sedatives and breakfast gathered weight in his bowels, so he got up and unplugged the IV, and damn the nurses, damn the pain… He made his way to the toilet by the nurses' desk. Normally his walking around without the drip trailing after him would get him an annoyed shout, but this time they didn't seem to notice his passing.

Trent sat down and relieved himself, then went to wash his hands.

He had no reflection in the mirror.

Stifling a scream, he scrubbed at his face, his chest, and felt they were solidly there.

But in the mirror was nothing.

Oh, it's the booze, it's the booze, he thought half-coherently, got to get help…

He staggered out into the corridor. None of the nurses looked up.

'Help,' he croaked. Still, nobody looked up.

Trent weaved over to his bed – he'd hammer the alarm, they couldn't ignore that – and this time was unable to suppress a scream that seemed to rupture his throat and eardrums.

He was lying in the bed; his lips were blue and caked in the residue of his breakfast. His face was white, his eyes black and glassy and sly. As he watched, the breakfast things were cleared from in front of the body, the woman not pausing to glance down at his immobile features.

He heard a voice over his shoulder.

In a chatty tone, the old man sitting on the bed next to his said, 'So then. About that electricity…'

A NICE POLITE LAD

It was a stupid mistake, the kind anyone in a hurry could make.

Rick had never stolen anything in his life, but when he half-ran out of the shop with the shaving foam and razor he realised he'd forgotten to pay.

He'd been too busy checking his watch, calculating how much time he had to get home, shave, shower, get to the wedding – then he passed between the sensors in the doorway and the whole department store was filled with a shrill, spiralling noise that sent three security guards after him like antibodies.

Everyone in the yellow-tiled stadium looked round, and he registered faces ranging from blank startle to spiteful satisfaction: another thieving little git caught by his own stupidity. The chilly air-conditioning and waft from the meat counter suddenly crowded in and the people walking by in the shopping arcade a few feet away and the shoe shops and opticians and travel agents all super-bright till he thought he might overload; might wet his pants.

The guard who grabbed him was barely older than him, or at least barely larger; an undernourished, sandy-haired youth in a blue uniform. 'It's alright, I'll do this one,' he called over his shoulder, and the other two guards backed off.

Rick's throat was too dry and narrow for speech; he held out the tin of shaving foam – sensitive skin brand – and expensive razors (four blades for extra closeness) and tried to shrug.

'Bit late to give em back chum,' said the youth – no, man; his narrow face was seamed and greyish. 'It's still stealing.'

Rick finally spoke. 'I just didn't want to be late, I forgot to pay.'

'Right.'

Rick dragged some crumpled notes out of his pocket, fighting an urge to say, Look, real money – not even a card! Real money! And how much to make you let go of my arm?

'See, I was going to pay for it…'

'Ye – es, but you didn't, did you? Is this too technical for you or what?'

'It was a mistake.'

'It certainly was, son.'

'No, I meant to pay but I've got to get somewhere really soon, in –' he showed his watch as if it might give added authenticity, 'well, not long now.'

'Court appearance, was it?'

Again, Rick looked around the store and tried to ground himself. He came here all the time; he lived down the road; he was part of the scenery. Except now there was a zone, a cone, of exclusion around him and the weedy man with pebble eyes and the radio mic clipped to his belt.

He shoved a breath past a lock in his breastbone, and said in a steady voice, 'No. My uncle's wedding. But I left it to the last minute, I was in a hurry and I'm happy to pay up or sign something or –'

'Not so easy, I'm afraid. You'll have to wait in the back while we call the police.'

'How long will that take?' said Rick, knowing it was an inane question even as it burst out.

'Generally with shoplifters, quite a while. Quite low down their list. But still…'

For a split second Rick considered asking one of the cashiers to vouch for him. But he didn't recognize any of them, and his loyalty card was at home. Would that do any good anyway?

Absurd as it was, it might've been worth a try. But it was at home, where he should be, shaving off his three-day stubble and changing out of the shabby clothes he'd worn for a quick trip to the shops.

'I am not a shoplifter,' Rick said slowly and clearly. 'I told you, it was an honest mistake.'

'An "honest" mistake, okay, I like that,' said the man, pushing him into the corner beside the doors. He smirked. 'Not a shoplifter, then. So what are you? What do you do for a living?'

The question was so odd that Rick was momentarily sure he might giggle. 'I'm sorry?'

'Bet you are, but what do you do for a living when you're not half-inching our merchandise?'

'I freelance. Computers.'

'Can you prove that? You're not just some slug on benefits?'

'Not right away. But I can make a call, you could speak to people I've worked for.' This could be an out: if he could prove he wasn't what the man thought he was, maybe he could walk away – My credit is good, kind sir. Rick allowed himself a small flash of contempt he kept carefully, deeply hidden: Take a look at my bank balance, Mister Three Pounds Fifty An Hour, see if you feel so superior then.

Then a strange thing happened.

The man let go of his arm and said, 'Okay, I think you're good.'

'Good...? Good to go?'

'Maybe. Tell you what, I'll overlook it this one time – as long as you pay up, then have that shave.' It was impossible to tell if the man was trying to be funny. 'But I'll be watching, so make sure you pay. Go on, hurry up.'

Rick fumbled his purchases into a plastic bag at the checkout in a blur, then walked out past the man with a grimacing smile.

As he was stumbling away into the noisy mall with a feeling of pure oxygen in his head, the man darted out after him and took hold of his arm again. God, what now?

Before he could speak, the man said, 'Tell you what, you're a good sort and I was out of order. I'll help you out. You're in a hurry, yeah?'

'Obviously.'

'Okay, well, there's a gents toilet, lavatory, just over there, you know where it is?'

What the hell was he driving at? 'Sort of.'

'If you're in a hurry, have your shave there. I'll put a sign outside, you know, cleaning in progress, so you won't be disturbed. Help you out.'

'I only live just over the road.'

'No, I've done you wrong, I want to see you right. Come on,

it's just here, look.'

The man steered him through a riveted metal door into a small washroom before he could protest. 'See? Nice and clean. No-one'll bother you. My treat.'

'But I – ' Rick looked round, but the man had already gone.

He was alone in a white, cramped space with a single cubicle, a small urinal, and a sink with a smeared metal mirror.

This wasn't right. It had to be some kind of joke.

The man was probably waiting outside, ready to radio for backup if the failed thief tried to bolt. Jesus, he might even inspect me to see if I've shaved, thought Rick, and laughed unsteadily, then glanced round.

The cubicle door was half open; he was definitely alone. Just get it over with, he told himself – after all, it *would* save a few minutes… It was silly – absurd, even grotesque – but why not? Ah, you people pleaser, he thought.

Then he splashed water on his face, lathered on the shaving foam and told the frightened eyes in the mirror that he'd have a laugh about this at the wedding reception in… Christ, he was late. Hurry up and get it over with.

He fitted a blade into the futuristic shaving tool and started on his neck.

He was half finished when the man came in.

'Nearly done I see. Sorry I was a bit harsh, like.'

'That's okay,' said Rick through a mouthful of foam. Humour the guy, perform this weird ritual humiliation or whatever it was, maybe even a clumsy act of generosity the idiot thought would make him feel better, and get out.

Nearly done.

'Have to be careful, you know.'

'I understand,' said Rick, scraping more quickly.

'Lots of druggies and shirt lifters try to use this convenience, you know.'

'I'm sure.'

'But I see you, shaving away…' He sounded genuinely contrite; perhaps he was hoping Rick wouldn't report him for his earlier heavy treatment.

'Look, we're cool. Don't worry about it.'

The man came and stood right behind Rick. 'Wouldn't it be easier if you took your shirt off? You'll get shaving stuff all down your collar.'

'It's fine. I'll be changing soon.'

'Will you? Still, no harm taking it off.'

Rick tried furiously hard to concentrate on the few remaining inches of stubble and not the intent eyes and smile just over his shoulder.

Suddenly the radio on the man's belt crackled and a voice emerged. 'Dempsey, respond,' it said.

'Oops. All go in this place,' said the man. He made no move to answer the radio.

'Dempsey, where are you? You're taking the piss. Respond immediately.'

'Shouldn't you answer that?' said Rick.

'Presently. Yes, lots of shirt lifters in here. I've got a caravan, you know.'

Rick nodded and scraped, nodded and scraped, cutting his chin. He wondered if he had strength in his legs to just walk out of the door right now.

'A nice caravan. When I'm there I like to do the old razzle dazzle.'

Rick froze. What...? What did that mean?

The radio spoke again. 'Dempsey, if you don't report to my office in two minutes you can find another job. Is that clear?'

Swallowing, Rick said, 'That sounded pretty urgent. Really, hadn't you better –?'

'Oh no. Dempsey's alright. He's just in there.'

The man pointed to the half open cubicle.

For the first time, Rick noticed the very edge of what looked like a brown shoe inside. Or perhaps a blue shoe with a red-brown, drying glaze splashed across it; it was hard to tell.

'So anyway, about the old razzle dazzle,' said the man. 'Dempsey didn't fancy it. But he got it anyway.'

He turned off the radio at his belt and pulled something from his pocket.

It took Rick a few long, creaking seconds to realise it was a switchblade.

WRONG MAN, WRONG PART

Ian Pascoe emerged from the shadow of an underpass, fumbling for a scrap of paper with an address on it.

The street was wide and featureless, full of fumes and din from the traffic. This had to be the place: the redbrick building on the far side had no number, but flaking white letters over the gate read T – B-RN S-REET ST-DIOS.

Ian waited for the green bead in the distance to go red, studying the building. Isolated on a patch of waste ground, it was dilapidated and grimy; an archway, a barred metal gate half open, and a cobbled tunnel beyond.

The traffic-light changed and he picked a way through the cars, exhaust blasting his legs in the cold air, heads staring.

Up close the studio complex looked almost derelict, surrounded by rubble and bin bags covered in curls of frost. In the growing dark, he saw an ugly patchwork of boarded windows and pocked brickwork; the cobbles were tracked with mud and litter. Through the gate Ian saw a white patch of wall and a door marked SECURITY, but the sliding window beside it was unlit. In a courtyard further back, a few shapes that must be parked cars glimmered. With cold hardening into the air, the silence and stillness felt very solid, very permanent; Ian wasn't surprised by his reluctance to step through the gate. He might have confused his dates or times; he stared at the bit of paper but it was too dark to read it.

This wasn't a nice area by any stretch, the kind of place ideal for getting mugged. There was graffitti all over the walls inside like luminous vines, and the cobbles were salted with broken glass.

No, he thought. This really doesn't look good.

Then facing the long walk back the way he'd come, Ian got an image of the rest of the evening, the rest of the week, if he left now. The closer to home he got, the more restless and frustrated he'd feel, until soon he'd be cursing his cowardice and another missed opportunity. Then the office and well-meaning questions, How was the audition Ian? He'd lie, then live through more months of boredom and resentment. Who knew what he might be missing just because his middle-class squeamishness flared up whenever he found himself somewhere slightly rough? Honestly, what a spineless milk-baby, he told himself. And this had looked so promising: a play, a troupe...

Ian pushed the gate wider.

The courtyard was large, with two more archways at the far end.

He wouldn't stumble about in the dark trying to find the room for long, he decided. Just a quick look.

Wondering if his background and upbringing, the urge to escape them, were about to lead him into trouble, he stepped into the courtyard. Then he saw someone watching him beside one of the archways. Ian flinched and had to stop himself bolting, but the figure made no move.

'Hello,' he said in a faint voice. 'I'm here for the audition. The actors' collective.'

No answer.

'Maybe you could tell me which room it is?'

No answer, and the figure no longer looked quite like a human outline.

'Listen, I don't have a phone number for them,' said Ian, moving forward. As he stared so hard his eyes prickled with cold, the more he thought he was talking to a shredded poster on the wall, or maybe a stain on the brickwork.

The white shape detached itself from the wall and walked away through one of the arches.

He fled.

Halfway along the street something occurred to him that made him stop and turn back.

Must be nerves that had kept him from realising sooner. He checked the note in the light of a shopfront – *7:15, Unit 38 (push buzzer)*.

He'd been early, so there was still time; he hurried back toward the studio.

As the building floated nearer, he had to laugh; he'd been close to throwing away a good chance by letting the security guard scare him off. That had to be what the white figure was who'd been watching him, naturally, and couldn't be bothered to talk to some weedy would-be actor; he must've been on his rounds, which explained the unlighted front office.

It was thirteen minutes past seven; Ian picked up the pace enough to heat his forehead despite the chill. This time, he wasn't going to back out for anything.

In the courtyard he stumbled between the half-seen cars and bins to the archway where the man had disappeared. A weak bulb halfway along the tunnel showed up an arrow-shaped sign on the wall. **Units 20 – 50**. Of course, the man had simply been showing him the way. Ian followed the arrow into a second pool of darkness.

Feeling his way along the walls, he came to a metal door. Its edges were white-hot with a seam of light, and squinting he picked out the numbers 21 – 30 painted above the handle.

The door opened inward with a croak. Inside was a passage of plain concrete, with an uneven string of lights threaded into the distance. Set into the grey walls were several kinds of door, some covered by bars or wire grilles, and a rainy smell mingled with cigarette-smoke filled the air. There were muffled noises further along – he thought he could make out sewing-machines, a band practising, muffled voices. One of the doors had a hand-lettered sheet of cardboard taped to it reading MINICAB'S, but other than that they were blank. How was he supposed to find the right room?

Ian studied the bells and intercoms by the first few doors, but these too were unmarked. Well, it had to be further along – made sense. Trying not to think of the time, Ian went further into the corridor. So poor were the lights that a black curtain seemed to retreat before him as he went; with each unmarked door his head pounded a little harder.

He came to a turning and checked his watch. Nearly twenty past; and all the noises were less distinct, but still somehow ahead of him. There was definitely activity somewhere, but looking back at the surprising distance he'd already covered, he couldn't pinpoint any of it. He turned the corner to another stretch of doors.

Somewhere ahead, one of them slammed.

For a moment the sound froze him, he wasn't sure why. Then he ran toward it, rounding another corner, and skidded to a stop when he saw another empty corridor, the lights trailing off around another bend. The echoes of the slamming door had faded beneath the thump and buzz of music somewhere, the gurgle of water in an overflowing sink.

'This is fucking ridiculous,' he said loudly, nearly shouting, then wished he hadn't. If one of these doors flew open, he wasn't sure how he'd react. It might be the right one; then again, it might not.

All at once, Ian had to get out. The bitterness and sense of failure, anger at the idiots who'd lured him here, all of that would follow as always; but for now, there was no way he could stay in this building. It was too late, anyway, though what for was no longer clear.

The doors sped past in strips, then he had to slow down. Not because he wanted to: because he was lost. He'd taken more turnings than he could possibly have been through on the way in. There must've been a junction somewhere he hadn't noticed properly – typical failure to keep his cool, he was too worked-up for an audition now anyway, best get out now, it was too late, too late…

One of the doors nearby rattled open.

A woman stepped into the corridor and looked him slowly up and down. She was very pale, skin almost matching the white of her dress where a silver brooch glimmered, a sickle or a waning moon, with black hair and black eyes glistening in a long face.

'You've come for the audition.' Her voice was sibilant and thin.

'…Yes,' Ian swallowed dryly. 'But I know I'm too late, sorry.' He made a placatory gesture and tried to sidle away.

'There's still time. You can come in.'

'I don't want to be any trouble.'

'Please.' She stepped back into the doorway without turning her back to him, edging out of sight.

Ian stared at the light streaming from the threshold. Did he feel lucky, or nervous, or both? Would he just walk past and keep going? He didn't know, but thought he was doing just that until he entered the room.

The woman was watching him, as were the group of four in a corner behind her. The sight of them, and the silence, made him babble. 'Look – I've changed my mind, I'm not really up for this.'

'But we waited for you,' she said.

'What, for *me*?'

'We've been waiting for someone we can really write.'

Ian smiled weakly. 'Write with? God, I'd love to do a script. Anything.'

'Here's a script for you.'

The light, the room, his whole body, seemed to stutter and flicker.

What was that?

Infinity, plenitude, the Alpha and Omega – transience, transit, serenity.

There was another stuttering, a flicker that slammed his ribcage.

Ian blinked. The pale woman and her four silent friends were smiling at him in the concrete room.

'I'm sorry,' she said, 'you didn't get the part, I'm afraid.'

He was too numbed to feel disappointment or anything else. 'If I'm not right for the part, I'm just not right.'

She nodded, reaching into her dress. 'No, you're not. Your final scene showed a distinct lack of character.' Then she produced a small, curved silver dagger and thrust it into his chest.

VERY PERSONAL HELL

'Play your music at this hour again and I'll call the police!'
The pimply, hooded youth from next door gave a threatening roll of his shoulders like a confused oarsman. 'Watch me go cube-shaped. You're locked in the toilet, knaa.'
The man stared, then spoke patronisingly. 'Sorry, I don't speak dickhead. Try English, little boy.'
'We give you fierce cactus lickings. Full and sinister.'
He made light of the threat, whatever it was. 'Jesus, are you propositioning me? I'm not subsidising your drug habits with bum-sex.'
'Verbals is mung and you is blood-bagged.'
'It's no good talking to me like a "rude boy", you rude little boy. I know you went to grammar school.'
At this point, an evil-smelling bucket of –

Kevin swore and crumpled up the printout. What a load of dross.

'It's useless,' he said to the empty flat, 'it's just not working. I don't have a clue. I don't know how teenagers speak and I don't fucking care. The promising little life-in-front-of-them cunts.'

Not a helpful situation – or attitude – for a would-be writer, he thought, reaching for his well-flogged pack of cigarettes. So think of a different idea, he told himself.

'I'm right out of ideas. That was the last one, it feels like.'

It had seemed so droll when he'd scribbled down the first vague notes – a humour piece about mismatched neighbours and their escalating war of loud music, suggested when the man living above him had taken to playing loud classical and opera, sickly jackbooted madrigals, and singing along when drunk. The thing was, he'd fallen silent recently, on holiday or perhaps moved away; after that, the irritation that powered the story had disappeared with him. All Kevin was left with was some second-hand social comment and a few lame gags, and the lees of the time he'd taken off work to be creative. The flats either side were vacant too – no more noisy sex from the left or random werewolf screaming from the right; the silence, the lack of a goad, seemed to have lulled his thoughts to sleep.

By association, he glanced at the half-full gin bottle on his desk.

'Fuck it,' he said to the collection of eighties centrefolds spread across the wall, 'let's get drunk. Here's to when bushes were mighty, tits were real, and I didn't have to work for a living because I was unhappily at school. Your very good health, ladies.'

As he filled his glass, there was a thump through the wall from the right-hand flat, as of moving furniture.

Boredom rather than any feeling for community made him look into the corridor. Next door was ajar, wedged by boxes, and he heard shufflings and mutterings from inside. Not quite sure why – but then he'd been stewing indoors for days – he took things further: he knocked, then poked his head in.

A shabbily-dressed man in late middle age was struggling to position a table in the middle of the room.

'Need a hand at all?' said Kevin.

The man turned. 'No thanks, but kind of you to...' He stopped and smiled.

Kevin stared.

The man's face was a haggard, seamed replica of his own, years older. 'Ah,' he said in a roughened version of Kevin's voice, 'there you are. I was wondering when I'd catch up with you – or vice versa.'

Kevin felt his limbs seize up, then suddenly go slack. '...Who are you?'

'I'd've thought that was obvious. Here, take a good look.'

'I don't understand.'

'You wouldn't, no. I, my friend, am the end product.'

'This is a... Is it a –?'

73

'It's no joke, sadly.'

'End product? Of what?'

'Years of alcohol abuse, social inadequacy and obnoxious selfishness.' The man – himself – beamed with malicious cheer. 'It's like *A Christmas Carol*, innit? Without the happy ending though, I'm afraid.'

So perfect and dreamlike was Kevin's sense of dread, of affront, that he found himself believing it. 'So what happens now you've found me?'

'Nothing.'

'Nothing? But what happened... will happen... to bring you here?'

'Again, nothing. Nothing at all. No drama: you go on with your life and eventually turn into me. End of story. You don't write anymore, by the way – I just can't be arsed, frankly. Oh,' he said before Kevin could protest, 'if only you knew. What's in store, I mean – which is very little. Bar the odd ups and downs, your life's going to be utterly uneventful and more than a little frustrating. But it's no so bad once you get used to the idea.'

'That's... horrible.'

'As I say, you'll learn.' As if to deepen the wound, the man added, 'mostly I like a bit of gardening and those programs about history, World War II and stuff – I've no complaints.'

'I won't have this. I won't.'

'I know. But that's beside the point.'

'You can't stay here – please.'

'Don't worry, you'll find I'm a very considerate neighbour. Just right for an aspiring thirty-something professional like you – regular hours, no vices, no rowdy social life... No strange women flouncing in and out... You'll hardly know I'm here.'

'How long have I got before – I mean, how old are you?'

'Fifty-five next April. Maybe we could have a joint birthday, a few cold ones down the pub.' The man grinned.

Kevin spent the next few days in a fog of alcohol. He stayed with friends, moving from person to person until his nervousness tired them all out – the old man had been right; his social circle was pretty small. Then he cajoled Natalie, an ex-girlfriend he hadn't seen for ages but had parted with reasonably amicably, to let him share her bed; she insisted on wearing hideous tartan pyjamas.

When he ran out of conversation and clean clothes, he tried going home.

With huge relief, he saw the next-door flat was unlit and quiet; perhaps, he thought, sinking into his chair and fumbling for the last inch of gin, the whole thing had been a waking nightmare brought on by overindulgence and lack of sleep, a spark from an imagination in burnout.

Then he heard noises from the other empty flat, the one to the left.

Quickly, to get it over with, he hurried into the corridor and found the left-hand door ajar. A scree of music, the kind he used to pretend to like, was playing quietly while a youth in a scuzzy T-shirt arranged oddly-shaped candles on a dresser. On the wall in the same spot Kevin had glossy pictures of naked women, there was a poster for an award-winning Hungarian science fiction film.

Even before the boy looked round, Kevin knew he'd be faced by his sixteen year-old self; what was unexpected were tears and a burst of invective loosed without preamble.

'I hope you're pleased with yourself, you horrible old fucker. You sicken me. You had to go and throw it all away, you oxygen thief – you sexist fucking herd animal, you've wiped your arse on my future! I hope you get –'

Kevin slammed the door and turned to run away.

On second thought – *esprit d'escalier* and all that – he reopened the door and snapped, 'Virgin.'

So it went on. The older man came back; he appeared to have nothing better to do than wander the town all day every day, whistling through his teeth. The youth made treks to the all-night service station and filled the corridor with skunk fumes, his stereo now cranked up to tinnitus-level; he appeared to have nothing else to do either, nor any friends. In many ways, the older man's attempts at banter were worse; the inane greetings and pretence of early senescence – at least, Kevin hoped it was a pretence – the long rambling diatribes, all very similar, about the council not picking up rubbish, the truancy and lawlessness of children…

Eventually Kevin phoned Natalie.

After a few strained preliminaries, he asked, 'Look, I know this'll sound like I'm taking the piss, but I'm really in trouble here. Could I come back? I'll sleep on the couch, the floor, in the bath, anything – just for a few days. Please… I'm at the end of my rope, I've got unbelievable neighbour problems…'

'You're really selling me the idea, honey bunny,' she said coolly. 'It might have helped your case if you'd made even a slight pretence of actually wanting to see me, or even pretending an interest – but that was never your strong suit. As it happens, I'm having neighbour problems of my own.'

'Yeah, fair enough, I'll try to be more…' he swallowed hard. 'Problems?'

'This mad old woman's moved in next door and keeps pestering me. I think she's just lonely and looking for sympathy – she's almost as bad as you, in fact. That, and she's clearly mad. It's doing my head in.'

'How so?'

'She keeps getting drunk and claiming to be me. On top of that, she –'

Kevin hung up.

The knock at the door, two cheery raps, came as he was packing his bags. He knew before opening it that he'd find the older man on the doorstep; and as Kevin snatched the door aside, suddenly aching for some kind of confrontation, for finality, there he was: thinning hair neatly plastered to his head, craggy face smiling.

'Not leaving us, I hope?'

'That's exactly what I'm doing, you poisonous old fart. Come on in, have your say – I might have a few words for you too – and then you can piss off.'

'Still quite impulsive, aren't we?'

'Do you mean "aren't we", or aren't *we*? Was that a feeble attempt at wit or are you really as retarded as you act?'

'There's no call for that sort of nastiness.'

'Jesus, am I going to suffer a head injury at some point in later life?'

'Well, I did say I was the end product – chalk it up to booze damage, brain rot. Your lifestyle's just shocking, you know. And for what?'

'For you, apparently.'

'Hmm.' The man smiled complacently. 'You can't say you weren't warned, either. Every step of the way, you ignored your parents –'

'You know, you sound a lot like them. It's disgusting.'

'Always knew better, didn't you? Always conceited, bad-tempered...'

'No, really. It's disgusting.'

'And you're not?' The man's smile tightened for a moment, a flash of animosity quickly smoothed over. 'When I think of you – of everything you wasted – all the time I'll never have back...'

'It's disgusting,' Kevin said again, voice rising to a shriek. Then he did something he'd wanted to do, wanted from an almost sexual depth, for a long time: he drove his fist into the man's face.

When nothing happened to him – the man, however, reeled back and slid halfway down the wall – all the caution and scientific superstition that had held him back fell away. He began kicking and punching the older man, knocking him down every time he tried to rise; soon he couldn't rise and lay curled in a ball, then flattened out and lay prone; Kevin kept on kicking until what lay there was no longer recognizable as himself, or anyone at all.

When he got back to the flat later that night, very drunk, he found it empty. There was no body, and the walls and floor were clean of blood.

He goggled at the place where the corpse had lain – but had the man been dead? Could he have...? Kevin struggled to formulate the scene past drink and shock. Maybe the boy next door had helped him...?

He raced into the corridor.

Both flats were open; both were empty, devoid of furniture, tracked with dust.

Kevin staggered back into his own flat and passed out.

It was dark when another knock sounded at the door, two cheery raps.

Kevin struggled half out of bed, squinting across the unlit room; had he remembered to lock the door before falling unconscious?

His chest hitched, seemed to lock without breath as the door began to open.

A green-black, decaying hand gripped the edge of the door, swinging it wider; in the sparse light of the streetlamp through the window, he somehow recognized the hand as his own.

THE PATH ENDS SUDDENLY

'No wonder they call it the Third World country of Europe.'

'Who? Your snotty friends no doubt. You're such a snob – and a whiner.'

Jon Powers tried to look contrite. 'Sorry, darling. I've got a hangover... I'm really suffering.'

'Me too.' Laura Powers tilted her chin, either in irritation or to blot him out in the flaring sun caught in her dark glasses.

They were halfway up a mountain in the crowded compartment of a funicular railway; soon they'd reach the top, walk around, take photos, find a café – and he could have the half-litre of beer he'd been thinking of since they'd left the hotel. He was bilious, his head was pounding and his heart was making alarming little jumps that caught his breath.

You're suffering, you bitch, he thought; I'd like that.

His jowly face was so slick with ill-smelling sweat it was all he could do to keep his own sunglasses from slipping off his nose – the shaky hands didn't help, nor the sun boring into his bald scalp. He felt confused and rudimentary, reduced to a thirsty, stupid animal. If the cabin hadn't been so full of chattering foreigners who evidently didn't understand the value either of quiet or deodorant, he'd have heaved open the door and pushed the fat old cow through.

Around them was nothing but hot blue sky and parched trees glued very thinly to rocky brown hills; far below, winding ravines, houses that seemed three quarters plastic sheeting and scrap iron.

Dogs barked, roosters hooted, and the press of Latin-looking gypsies around them foghorned and gestured and jostled. Bastards. His guts quaked, not gently, and he let go a silent but brutal fart with malicious pride.

They were nearly at the top of the steep rail cut into the cliff-side; the small train groaned, shuddered, and his knees were briefly thrown against Laura's. They recoiled simultaneously, without comment.

Once the door had ground open they waited for the crowd to disperse, used the flyblown public toilets and stood at the parapet overlooking the town and sea for some minutes, unspeaking.

'Now what?' Powers said at last. The sight of the oil-refineries and rows of identical red-tiled roofs, their dullness, made him feel like screaming obscenities into the hills.

'You'll be wanting a drink, I imagine,' said Laura. She'd been very pretty once, but now she looked beaten-down, bored and bitter – first a subtle, then a not-so-subtle alteration that was mainly his fault, he supposed.

Still, he'd had his disappointments too. This shitty budget holiday paramount among them right now, he thought; so in a sneery voice he said, 'You divine correctly as ever, my sweet. Let's see if we can find one before we *both* end up sulking, shall we?'

'You're the boss,' she said with a rather pathetic irony that infuriated him.

Jesus, just where had they lost the path? When had all this become the norm?

Oh forget it, he thought. I want that beer, especially if there's a long walk after. Another of her stupid ideas. Does she want to give me a coronary?

As he shouldered his small bag with sun cream, beta blockers, insect repellent and digital camera (but no water), he decided he didn't much care. And he also decided, 'Let's just get going. I can wait for a drink. You'll see.'

On the first half hour of their walk up through the hills, the greenery unexpectedly broadened and deepened and became quite beautiful. Absorbed, he stared down the steep path they'd climbed into the dense trees and said, 'It's like one of those paintings, you know, that German Romantic bloke – Caspar David Friedrich.'

She purred and knew exactly what he meant and for one of the moments that had been frighteningly scarce recently he felt very close to her. Powers touched her shoulder gently and Laura rested against him.

'Worth it after all?' she said.

'Absolutely,' he answered with no hesitation or fakery at all. At the same time, he thought: There's no-one around for miles. I could give her just one little push...

He glanced down into the scarp of snarled branches, thorns and rocks below and shuddered. No, he thought in a voice that resonated through him. Be kind. Be more patient. Just... try harder.

She smiled at him in the most unforced way he'd seen in weeks and he felt strong and good. 'Let's carry on,' he said. 'We'll find somewhere back in civilisation to have lunch.'

It took them perhaps another twenty minutes to realise they were lost.

The rich landscape had been supplanted by a narrow, crumbling path next to a dried-up canal. Sometimes the path was concrete, sometimes loose stones, sometimes mud. The stones and mud shifted nerve-tighteningly – the path was only ten inches wide, often a little less. On one side was a channel full of weedy, stagnant puddles and refuse. On the other was a sharp drop into dusty fields, several miles below.

Panting, his heartbeat playing an unfamiliar rhythm high in the walls of his throat, Powers said 'Hold on a sec, please. Can we look at the map?'

Laura dug out the guidebook from her money-belt.

Considering his anxiety, Powers thought he did a good job of keeping the exasperation from his voice. 'No, the other one from the hotel. They said it had all the tourist paths on it.'

Laura fished out the other map, a glossy flag of paper that had cheerfully led them wrong before, and squinted at it. 'It's not on here,' she said flatly.

'What isn't? Am I a fucking mind-reader? *What* isn't?'

'Wherever we are... Although...'

'Although what?'

'That there. Actually, I think maybe that's where we are; we must've missed the signs.'

'Signs where?'

'Back on the first bit. There'd have to be, because I think that blob there stands for "roadworks". Or it could be "earthworks". Look at the canal – it's completely dry.'

'Yes, I noticed that some time ago.'

'But why is it dry?'

It was a three-foot groove through twigs and mulch, floored with what looked like recently-laid cement. He also realised he could smell diesel fumes and, far off, hear the buzz of machinery. 'Well, let's turn back then,' he said.

'All that way? What about my hip and your ankles? Look, if something dangerous was being done they would've warned us at the terminus.' She marched ahead.

'They have different standards here,' he bleated, then realising how pathetic and xenophobic he sounded, he hurried over the uneven ground to belie his words, his indecision, by catching her up.

They passed the first workmen soon after, bony-faced young men in fluorescent jackets who fell silent as they struggled over the planks cluttering the walkway. The canal was now blocked off with struts of bleeding green wood, and bales of barbed wire stamped down the undergrowth. The wine and roar of machines was everywhere but impossible to pinpoint; greasy smoke drifted across the path.

'Maybe we should ask one of these men if we're going roughly the right way,' said Laura, but without enthusiasm.

They high-stepped over a mass of ashes. 'I hope we are,' snapped Powers, 'I've seen enough of this country's light industry and dammed canals.'

'Oh, shut up.'

'Not to mention logging,' he cut in. 'Listen. That's a saw of some kind, a chainsaw, isn't it? They're chopping down all the trees too. Surely that's illegal up here. It's a conservation area.'

'So now you're an ecology expert,' she said, amused at his aggrieved tone – except she wasn't. He could hear fright in her voice.

There were piles of bleached timber by the path where it plunged into the trees, and the heaps of cinders seemed to grow larger with each they passed. They rounded another bend and walked through another pack of silent, appraising workmen. The machine-noise was very loud now, the smoke very thick.

'Please let's go back,' said Powers.

'Come on, it's only another fifteen minutes at most,' Laura said through gritted teeth.

'But the map's wrong,' said Powers as he trailed after her.

They wound through another narrow ribbon of path, then stopped. Ahead was a flight of three moss-covered concrete steps. Beyond was a workman blocking the path, pushing a wheelbarrow slopping over with wet cement. The slender space to his left was piled with more of the stuff in a porridgey mound, ready to be tipped into the canal.

'He'll help us through,' said Laura with a confidence he wished he could believe in, striding forward.

Powers matched her stride and felt better when he saw the plank gangway laid over the semi-solid mound of cement. Taking the lead, he smiled at the workman's impassive leathery face, took the hairy hand extended to help him onto the plank and across to the clear path. The workman's grasp was dry and strong and took a surprisingly long time to release. He lifted Powers over the plank and didn't let go. Instead, he began to push sideways.

Powers heard Laura scream and then felt her head crash painfully into his ear as they were both thrown into the canal. The wind knocked out of him, Powers watched as the workman began shovelling the cement in slippery globs – they fell on him and Laura, miring them and weighting them down as they lay in the canal; then the wheelbarrow was brought forward and its contents tipped over them, closing over his sight and then his breath.

SLAVES OF THE MUMMY

My old man was Jimmy Hall, so I don't expect to be believed right away. Journalism's in my blood – and it was in his, till it got splashed across some smelly country pub floor over that Quatermass business. Still, a certain reputation attends, if you know what I mean; you certainly will when I've finished. So listen.

If I weren't an alcoholic, this story wouldn't have happened and I wouldn't wake up post-nightmare every three a.m. trying to make sense of it, but anyway it started prosaically enough.

I was on punishment detail, to cover the launch of something called *England*. That's it, just *England*, and it was as vague and pretentious as the title and people involved would lead you to expect: ageing Brit Art celebs and their popstar mates, all with greying temples, growing jowls and newly-bought tweed suits. They'd stopped being cute or interesting nearly two decades ago and were looking for some gravitas, so they were solemn enough, although I'm still foggy on what it was all about – some sort of multimedia "installation" or glorified gig, probably.

What made it interesting from my point of view was the other person involved. A black Hollywood actor, still just about a star and not renowned for Anglophilia. Maybe he had a movie to promote and his agent somehow crowbarred him in, or maybe he really liked England: anyhow, he was on the skids or very close. I've no idea, and had no time to form any in the short but intense period we were acquainted – at first mainly because he was chasing me down the street trying to beat me senseless.

The launch was in one of those smallish Soho members' clubs, the media-specific places behind anonymous doors round the Square, the ones that are never quite as slick and toney as they like to think. Why not a gallery, a rock venue or night-club, I didn't know or care; maybe not serious or "English" enough, and besides it was easier to get served. The drink was free, so the snotty bar-staff and way most of the *artists* kept blanking me weren't so annoying at first, even in my grey mood. I wasn't mad keen to waste time talking to some poxy old drummer about his trout farm and Mister Hollywood hadn't shown up, so fuck 'em. Wankers. I shipped a lot of booze – I'm getting on, I need the fuel. I looked around the greenish room, sneering and sneered at, and grew steadily more drunk.

When the actor arrived I was taken by surprise, not least as he had no entourage and pitched up right next to me at the bar.

'Bodyguards got the night off?' I said, trying for a light conversational tone but maybe just sounding sarcastic; he flickered a half-glare at me, then all the barmen and girls were fawning over him. This gave me time to study him as carefully as my blurring vision allowed. Chris Elmore Holmes, a handsome man and in very good shape for his age (late thirties, early forties?). You'll have seen some of his godawful films, either the sensitive shit where he plays a concerned inner city teacher or drug dealer trying to go straight, or the noisy shit where he's a psycho cop with a big attitude – or some of the straight-to-DVD stuff he was forced to make later. He was muscular, well-dressed, more voltage than any of the chattering nonentities around him. Once they'd calmed down and dispersed a bit, I tried to get a word in.

'How often do you shave your head to get it that smooth?'

This time he fixed me with an undivided scowl.

'Don't get me wrong,' I said quickly. 'It looks great, but it must be really high-maintenance. That and trimming the beard.'

'I don't know you.' His voice was low and charged, just like in his films.

'Oh, I'm a journalist. Old school.'

'And I don't want to know you. And I don't want to talk to you.'

'But what about *England*?'

His deadpan didn't waver. 'What about it?'

'I mean this art... thing. *England*, you know, not the country.'

'I know what you mean.'

'I suppose they asked you along for an outsider's, a visitor's perspective,' I faltered, not immediately noticing when he called me a racist fucking hack under his breath.

'You think I've never been to London before?' He was turning away, about to dismiss me.

'There's more to England than London, you know. Granted, most of it's either deadly dull or quite shitty, but still, you should try stepping out of your Hollywood bubble occasionally.'

That got his attention. When he swung back to face me, it was a shade closer than before. 'I'm not ignorant, I'm not babied day and night. Why do you think I'm here?'

'Mister Holmes, that's what I'm trying to establish. Is it those crappy Brit horror remakes you're stuck doing now?' I was needling him, true; I'm not extra-nice when drunk. 'What was the last one? *Vampire Triggaz* – what a turkey. Well, Hammer House is nearby anyway.'

'I'm not here to be roasted by some rude old lush who can't even stand up straight.'

He was nearly shouting, and this pushed all my own – admittedly rather sensitive – dials into the red. 'Don't brush me off. I'm one of the little people, yeah. Well if you hadn't tanked your career you wouldn't be here sucking up publicity in the first place. And when you're on the way down, you fucking take care round those little people, because they'll –'

He moved closer still, with narrowed eyes. 'What's your name, boy?'

'Don't try that stone killa from Compton act with me. You went to Harvard, so fuck you and your fraud credibility. Go arse-creep the other frauds.'

At this point, he grabbed me.

My shirt popped buttons and my drink slopped over my shoes. 'Do what you like to me, but don't ever spill my drink,' I shrilled.

'Spill your blood, motherfucker.'

'That'll look great on the networks. I thought you were showing off your fake arty side, not the fake gangsta shit. You actor pussy.'

He threw a punch. It would've hurt a great deal had it connected, but by now someone had looped an arm round his wrist, deflecting his fist from my face by millimetres. There was a lot of jostling and shouting and I was hustled to the door by staff with acne and puppy fat.

'Boring evening anyway,' I shouted as they pushed me into the street. 'Full of boring people, like that sad case there,' and I pointed at Holmes. I thought myself safe, as he was blocked off by sycophants; I was wrong. He burst free of the knot of people and charged out after me.

'You're a dead cocksucker,' he yelled, gaining fast.

I've been beaten up in the course of my work a few times, but rarely in public and still haven't acquired a taste for it; so I really poured it on, but it was late and I was tired and out of condition. I was also too old and compromised with lager and Jameson's, so by now I was finding it hard to breathe and Holmes was only a few feet behind me. In a couple of seconds he'd be pummelling me into the wet evening pavement.

So I decided to hide.

We were somewhere in the small but complex tangle of side streets just off Soho's main drag – which worried me, as there was nobody about and so no witnesses or potential saviours (as if). In the drizzle and shadow I got a half-glimpse of flat-blocks, backs of department stores, a few posh offices – and a huddle of indeterminate structures with an open door right in the middle.

I ran inside. No good; I could hear Holmes pounding after me. Nevertheless, I stopped and stared.

'Get ready, you fucking sleaze –' yelled Holmes. Then he, too, stopped and stared at the place we'd found.

This is where it starts getting really weird.

I'd never seen anything like this and please God never will again, although I expect to revisit it in dreams for some time to come, among other things. It looked like we'd stumbled into an indoor amusement park, or more a giant ghost train ride. It was hard to guess the dimensions of the building – high cobwebby girders, a dusty concrete floor – because it was just a shell housing the structure that filled most of the space and gave off all the light. A lot of light, a sickly mingled glare of orange and green and red, lanced with flashes of blue and yellow. There was the entrance to a tunnel, a wooden archway carved into grotesque, irregular shapes. The tunnel was in darkness, but tracks ran across the floor into it and waiting on the tracks was a chair painted in equally gaudy, clashing colours, its shape as senseless as the vast construction about to swallow it. What really disconcerted me were the words picked out in pink neon above the arch. THUG LIFE CARNIVAL, they read, and below that in smaller bulbs: GHETTO GHOSTS.

'What *is* this?' Holmes said beside me, almost civil.

Once I'd got my wind back, I said 'No idea. If one thing it means is you're less interested in beating seven shades of shit out of me, I'm all for it. Whatever it is.'

He gave me a cold, considering glance.

I gave him one back – the alcohol and adrenaline still burning through me helped, and I used to be a bit handy when I was younger. Which is why I got reckless and said, 'Tell you what. Let's take a closer look, then if you still feel like doing me over, be my guest. I can't run any further or I'll throw up.'

Holmes curled his lip, then started toward the arch without a word or look my way. I let him get a few feet ahead, weighing up bolting while his back was turned, but then he looked round expressionlessly and waited for me to catch up. Besides, hideous as the ghost train was – the lights and colours hurt the eyes, ran together in an oily, queasy way – it was fascinating too, and perhaps unique. A story? A paragraph, anyway.

So Holmes and I approached the carriage, hesitated, then sat down at the same moment. Instantly, the carriage rattled into the tunnel, too quickly to jump off, and the lights outside were snatched away by a switchback into utter dark.

'Can you believe this shit?' said Holmes, voice harsh and loud in the confined cabin and near-silence. The only sounds were the mutter of the rails, now curiously muted, and a sense of air rushing past narrow walls.

'It could be a new attraction they're testing out, a secret.' I made little effort to sound convincing or conceal my unease.

'Who's "they"?' Holmes was talking more quietly, anxiously even.

'I don't know – a big computer-games conglomerate going retro. An eccentric millionaire. Aliens. Look, this was a bad idea

– let's try and get out.'

'I'm down wid dat,' he said in a mock-gruff takeoff of one of his tougher roles. It made me warm to him for an instant – just before the carriage turned another corner.

Weak grey light suggested a large room of crumbling brick, with windows and doorways in the walls. Figures moved quickly and furtively around the ill-lit space.

The carriage slowed almost to a halt, and it became obvious the figures were aware of us. A small boy in a hooded top appeared beside me. He had a puffy, dead-white face and sunken eyes.

'Hi mister,' he said in a piping whisper. 'Okay if I stab you now?'

He raised a switchblade toward my throat and I shook my head in a convulsion, gasping something unintelligible.

'Oh well. Some other time,' said the boy. With no change of expression at all he gazed at the knife for a moment, then stuck it deep into his own chest. As he fell, the carriage moved on.

'What the Christ was that?' Holmes choked. 'Was that animatronic or something?'

I looked back, biting down nausea, but the body and much of the room were already lost in dimness. We were nearing another corner, and the carriage dipped toward a glistening black door.

We both cried out, blinded by the sudden upsurge of light as we crashed through. There was a jolt, and the carriage stopped.

'Is that it? Are we back outside?' said Holmes, eyes shielded from the dazzle.

'No,' I said when I could make out where we were.

This room was huge, every corner picked out in flaring whiteness. Walls, floor and ceiling were gleaming marble; staircases and pillars receded into the distance. The room was full of people. They drifted at random, near and far, and the sight of them froze me with helplessness and fear. I looked behind us to see the black door had been replaced by a spot-lit wall. The rails too had vanished, and as we sat in the immobilised carriage some of the people began to inch toward us. There was a groaning, grey-fleshed man in a suit of rotting sackcloth; there was a creature, female, in a form-fitting green dress that matched its skin; above the anguished human smile it had the flat eyes of a snake. There were other things, shapes, one of which kept breaking apart into blurred multiple images before settling back into one; things I could make no sense of. But worst of all was the red-headed girl.

She was slender and pretty, with long curling hair and a white gown. She was murmuring to herself as she advanced, and as she came closer I saw her eyes were black and icy; her teeth were filed into points. As she murmured, a trickle of viscous yellow liquid escaped the corner of her mouth and she wiped it away with one bare arm. The other arm hung limp at her side as if paralysed. I knew if she raised that arm and touched me with it, something horrible would happen; my soul would be petrified inside me. Her voice was low and soft and sweet, its chanting lulling and compelling, almost making human sounds. There was a cold thread of mockery and greed underneath, and her insect eyes widened as she came close enough to reach out her dead Gorgon's arm.

Holmes shoved me out of the carriage and dragged me to my feet. 'We have to move,' he shouted.

'Where? There's nowhere to go.'

The girl was gliding around the carriage after us, and the other figures were closing in.

'Might be another door at the far end. We have to try.'

I let him lead me in a staggering run through the hall of figures. Some ignored us, some moved to block our path and take hold of us, muttering and giggling. They were slow, almost preoccupied; they knew there was no way out. We weaved through them and there, finally, was another arch ahead. I stopped.

Holmes grabbed my shoulder and screamed at me. 'What the fuck's wrong with you? We need to go! Can't you see that doorway?'

He was spraying me with an acrid mist of spittle and fear; as I replied, I did the same. Our spoor – and the creatures behind would follow it.

'Yes I can see the bloody doorway: I can't tell what's on the other side yet though. We're being herded.'

'You're a fool,' Holmes snarled.

I looked back. The figures wandered after us and the dead-armed girl was leading them; beside her were two identical girls, all three murmuring. I could almost understand their voices now, and somehow this decided me.

'You win,' I croaked.

We sprinted through the archway into a much smaller room.

Again, it was brightly lit in white marble, but in the centre of the floor were several urns of dull stone. Between the urns rested a sarcophagus in which lay a bundle of twigs and desiccated, unravelling vine leaves just recognisable as a mummified corpse. Some impulse – rage, cornered terror, perversity – made me kick over one of the urns. It smashed into countless fragments and spilled a cargo of ashes and withered preserved organs across the floor. A moan of pain or distress wafted from the sarcophagus.

'That's it,' I said, 'they want to feed us to that thing.'

Holmes stared at me, then at the crowd gradually building outside the arch. 'Is that why they're mostly women out there? Like his mother?'

'Or his bitches? Oh, you sexist.'

'Bigot,' he said distractedly.

'No, they're more like...' More like an alliance, I thought with fear-sharpened intuition. An alliance of monsters.

Holmes crossed to the bier and reached into his jacket. 'Okay,' he said, voice cracking, 'let's see if we can do a deal.'

'Do a –? You're not in LA, you prick.'

'I mean keep them off.' He took a gold Zippo out of his pocket and, holding it over the sarcophagus, flicked the wheel.

The girl's voice was embedded quite clearly and understandably in my head now, lilting but with a hint of panic. **You must not harm him. He is the first and finest of us, the most untainted. Only he can lead. He is noble. If you do not harm him, we will allow –**

I heard a cry of pain.

'Shit,' said Holmes, the flaming lighter dropping from his burnt fingers into the dried-out remains.

'You idiot,' I screamed – a sheet of fire leapt from the sarcophagus and filled the room with bitter, cinnamon smoke.

When the smoke thinned, the room was gone. We were standing in a rainy London street as a bus hissed past.

We looked at each other blankly for a long time.

'Never mind,' I said when I was able to speak. 'If you're prepared to forget all that nasty stuff I said earlier, I'll buy you a new lighter.'

Holmes is still an actor, although as predicted his career's a little sub-par nowadays. He got involved in one of those spacey fringe religions, which can't have helped his credibility; maybe it just helps him, holds him together.

Me, I'm still an alcoholic – that's my defence, or excuse. I dream of crowds of people, or things like people, standing watching me in my bedroom in the dark. They're silent, but I feel their malevolence; I can't move or cry out.

WE KNOW WHERE YOU LIVE

'No,' said Wallace, shoulder wedged against the door, 'I'm not letting you in.'

'That's inadvisable, sir. We are authorised to inspect the premises.'

'So you keep saying. First of all, I want to see some ID.'

The thickset, greying man on the doorstep glanced at his colleague, a tall thin ginger-haired man, both of them dressed in dark green, and they shared a minute head-shake in disbelief at this piece of impertinence.

The first man began what sounded like a rote speech. 'I have explained the situation, sir, but if you insist I can attest that we are accredited officers of the Axial Emissions Authority, and are obliged...'

'I don't care. I'm not budging and this door doesn't come off the chain till I've seen some proper identification. And once you've done that, perhaps you can "explain" exactly who the Axial Emissions Authority are.' Wallace was careful to keep his tone quiet and his language moderate; God knew what they might be allowed to do if he started shouting and swearing, much as he wanted to.

'Very well, sir. Let's not make this any more difficult than necessary.'

Who, you two or me? thought Wallace, watching as the man reached into his jumpsuit. Again, he bit his lip. Just find out what these clowns wanted and, if possible, send them on their way.

Besides, the other one was hanging back silently and watching him, as if calculating how far Wallace could be induced to cooperate. 'A little closer please. I can't see it properly if you just wave it like that.'

The man steadied and raised the card by a fraction of an inch. It was still hard to read, but nothing could have made Wallace put his hand out to take it for a proper look; he had a ridiculous but strong feeling that if he did, they'd grab hold of his arm.

The card was thick white plastic, a blurry photograph in one corner, a logo, a string of what looked like numbers.

'That's not very helpful. It doesn't seem to give me your name, for instance.' It was getting harder and harder to keep the sarcastic bite out of his voice, a sarcasm that could quickly tip over into outright hostility. 'I'm closing the door now. If you're still outside in one minute – no, half a minute – I'm calling the police. Clear?'

'I'm glad you mentioned the police, sir. I must inform you that if you do not admit us to the premises, we are empowered to return in due course with a police officer, who will have a search warrant.'

'Then you can go do that, for all I care,' said Wallace, and slammed the door.

As he watched through a corner of the curtains, the men shrugged and got into a dark green van whiskered with aerials. They sat in it for a moment, studying a clipboard, then drove away.

When they came back two days later, Wallace let them in.

'I'm glad you've decided to be reasonable, sir.'

'It looks like I don't have much choice. I checked up on you people –'

The man frowned. 'Did you not read the letters? We've been sending you notifications for several months about inspections in your area.'

'I thought they were junk mail. Binned them. I'm too old to waste my time on form letters and rubbishy brochures.' Wallace suppressed any note of apology in his voice. Besides, they were just standing on the doormat letting in a cold breeze, and failing not to be obvious they were giving his hallway the once-over.

'But they're clearly marked as official correspondence, sir.'

'So's most junk mail nowadays. You might try a more efficient way of getting in touch with people.'

The second man looked momentarily offended, but still said nothing.

The other, who'd clearly heard this before, said 'A visit with a search warrant or a court order would've been even more official, sir. It's always nice when we don't need to go that far.'

'Just come in and stop wasting my heating, will you. For your information, I called the police. They weren't very helpful, so I told them I'm certainly going to complain about your heavy-handed way of carrying on. It must be borderline illegal.'

The front door clicked shut and they crowded into the hallway. The second man glanced down at the small telephone table and studied the mail spread out on it.

Another rote speech from the grey-haired man. 'There are channels available to you if you wish to make a complaint. Firstly...'

'Never mind all that now: but don't think I've forgotten either. Just get on with it. I assume you know what you're looking for.'

The man grunted as if this were unworthy of comment and they all walked toward the living-room.

'Live alone, sir?' The deadpan way this was said somehow made it seem an insinuation.

'Not that it's any of your business, but yes, my wife and I divorced a year ago.'

'And she left you the axial converter, did she? Very generous.'

'Look, what is an axial converter?'

Both men stared at him for a full and very heavy five seconds, maybe ten. Then the spokesman said, 'By law, every household's axial converter has to be checked for non-phase emissions. Every household has one.' It was as close to expression as his voice had yet come; and the tone told Wallace, Don't try and be funny.

'They're usually in here,' said the man, sniffing in a satisfied way as they entered the living-room and looked around.

'I'm perfectly serious,' said Wallace. 'Will you please explain to me what an axial converter is? Is it part of the electrical wiring, part of the fabric of the house, what?'

With a yet more obvious effort at staying poker-faced, the man said, 'Please let's not waste time, sir. We hear all kinds of bizarre excuses in this job. You'll be telling us you don't have one next.'

'But I'm sure I don't.'

The second man spoke for the first time, reedy-voiced and sour with triumph. 'What's that, then?' He pointed into a corner.

In the corner was something Wallace had never seen before.

It was about four feet high, a translucent bright blue egg, glowing softly and regularly. The pulses of light seemed to ripple the walls around it.

'I... I don't know,' said Wallace. 'I swear to you I don't know what that thing is. It wasn't there a minute ago.'

Secure in his rightness, the first man now let his voice drop a few notches toward insulting, while his colleague grinned. 'Come off it, sir. Like the ad campaign says, You Can Try, But You Can't Deny. And I must say, that's got to be the most feeble excuse of the lot. You'll still have to pay the fine, but that's a matter for the magistrates.'

Before Wallace could respond, both men crouched before the glowing object and brought out hand-held meters and screwdrivers. 'Now let's check this beauty.'

'Emissions, you said,' Wallace suddenly realised.

'That's what it's for,' the first man snapped, all pretence at patience dropped.

'But what kind of emissions?'

'Good ones, obviously. Unless they're non-phase, which, you'll be glad to hear, it looks pretty much like yours aren't.'

'I still don't understand. What emissions?'

Both men straightened up, dusting off their hands. 'It's a bit late to be playing the innocent,' said the spokesman.

'But I don't...' Wallace made a gesture half surrender, half denial. 'I don't want it, whatever it is. Switch it off.'

'We can't do that,' said the second man incredulously. 'Don't be crazy. Have you any idea what'll happen?'

'I don't care. Switch it off.'

The men silently consulted for a moment, then the spokesman produced a notepad. 'Individual requests disconnection of converter. Duly noted, time, date, fair warning given, blah blah blah. Okay then.'

He nodded to the other man, who went and did something to the top of the blue egg.

Everything stopped.

'Got the date-stamp?' asked the spokesman.

His workmate nodded and produced a rubber stamp and inkpad. The other man took it, stamped the page he'd written, then walked over to a man-shaped darkness prone on the carpet.

He angled the icy-cold neck carefully, then stamped the date on the yielding black ellipse where Wallace's forehead would have been. The numerals glowed there luminously.

The men let themselves out of the house.

SLIMECULT, OR -
WRONG MAN, WRONG PART: II

VOICE-OVER
It's the near future. There's been a disaster. A disaster only one
man can stop – and that one man *is* Ian Pascoe as SERGEANT
RAY BACKUS, LAPD. Nobody knows why the disaster
happened. But it did. And now, most of the world is covered in...
The Red Slime.

SCREAMING crowds in London – Big Ben, bowler hats –
running away from a tide of glistening red jelly.

Cut to: Paris (Eiffel Tower, berets), then Tokyo, Delhi.

Cut to: the world spinning in space, overwhelmed by red slime and
glowing faintly.

V/O
All except one place: Los Angeles.

Pounding MUSIC – palm trees, freeways.

V/O
But even there, there *is* a problem.

MUSIC turns queasy.

V/O
For reasons nobody understands, many of the city's population
have lost their heads. It may be the smog, it may be The Slime. In
fact, it *is* The Slime. But how? One man means to find out –
whatever it takes.

MUSIC turns to horror glitch-stabs.

EXT. LOCATION – DAY
Camera pans from a neon beer sign to a panicked group fleeing a
bar.

V/O
These lost souls are now the headless dead. They can only be
recognized because they have no heads.
A group of shuffling headless zombies stumbles out of the bar and
into a plaza where more are congregating, flailing and lurching.

V/O
But with his Ninja training, Ray Backus is here to stop them.
Crash-zoom to IAN PASCOE, stepping out of a patrol car in
police uniform. He flexes an eyebrow grimly.

IAN
(American accent)
Halt! Police, assholes!

The zombies shuffle on regardless, destroying buildings. Ian races
among them and with a series of CGI-assisted somersaults and
roundhouse kicks, knocks them all to the ground where they lie
twitching.

V/O
Ray Backus is a man with nothing to lose, and he won't rest till this
zombie menace is ended and The Red Slime is history.

Ian handcuffs a prone zombie and recites the Miranda into its neck cavity.

INT. LOCATION, PRECINCT OFFICE – DAY
Ian sits with his wisecracking Latino partner VASQUEZ as they
efficiently clean and load their handguns.

VASQUEZ
So she says... get this man... "I don't hardly never see you no
more – you're married to the friggin' job." Madre de Dios! You
believe that shit, man? Crazy thing is, I ain't fuckin' married to her
neither.

Bespectacled FAT MAN in sweaty shirt runs in.

FAT MAN
Backus, Vasquez, you gotta get movin' real quick. We got a 9-544-
1 from the dispatcher about that red goo. There's some crazy ice-
cream vendor at the Zoo, selling it to kids – turning them into
those zombies! Christ, he's even giving it to the fucking *animals!*

Strapping on of utility belts and CLICK-CLACK of weaponry.

IAN
Let's roll.

EXT. LOCATION – DAY

SCREAMING tires, SIRENS – police car leaps over a speed-bump
in a shower of sparks.

EXT. LOCATION, ZOO – DAY

The ICE-CREAM VENDOR wears a bizarre costume. Beaming,
he hands out tubs of poisonously-shimmering red ice-cream to a
crowd of happy kids.

Ian leaps out of car and into martial arts crouch.

IAN
Stop right there, mister!

(pause)
Hey, wait a minute… I know you…

VENDOR
(evil laughter)
That's right, buddy. It's me, the old pal who killed your wife and son. And now it's your turn.

Ian's head falls off and rolls into the gutter. He starts blundering around. The Vendor disappears in a flash of light. The kids run away SHRIEKING and Vasquez belatedly steps into view, then with a regretful grimace BLASTS Ian in the back with a shotgun. Blood-spray obscures the lens.

ROLL CREDITS

IT IS WRITTEN

Searching the apartment block for other survivors, Banks found Mrs Crofter weeping and struggling with the door of her flat.

He felt a little like weeping himself, but only a little; the three horrible hours since he'd woken and seen what had happened to his parents had tamped his emotions down into a hard ball. He started forward. 'What's wrong? Can I help?'

She gave him a distracted glance. 'My daughter's in there,' she said through tears, rattling the door handle.

Banks flexed his shoulders as he stepped up to the door. 'And you want to get her out.'

Now her eyes were glassy and round, and she gripped his arm. 'No! I want her to stay inside.'

As she quickly replaced her hand on the door and braced it against the keyplate, Banks realised the door was jolting outward, its lock broken. Mrs Crofter was trying to hold it shut.

'So she's...'

'Like all those poor people in the street,' said Mrs Crofter, the last three words a low scream as the door gave a lurch and nearly spilled open.

Banks took hold of the handle and tried to lock his knees, shoes squeaking on the cement floor. 'I'll hold it, you make a run for the stairs,' he said through gritted teeth.

She might not have heard him – she stared at the shivering door, biting down on her lip. 'I've been out here since twelve o'clock,' she said. She was small and elderly for a fifty-something, and Banks wondered how she'd managed to keep the door shut for an hour. 'Rachel was alright earlier. Then those things flew in the window… A big cloud of them… And they stuck to her…'

'Look – you have to go for the stairs. The lifts aren't working. I think this door's about to come off its hinges.'

The door shuddered under a sudden powerful blow; its upper half sagged out of the frame with a creak.

'She wasn't as strong before,' said Mrs Crofter in a choked voice. 'There must be more of them in there. Sticking to her and making her heavier.'

'We should get out of here. I'm sorry, but whether you come with me or not I'll –'

A few more seconds and he'd have to let go and run. The woman had plainly cracked; perhaps she'd clung to mind and spirit in the dark corridor as grimly as to the door, and his arrival had shattered her control. She was still staring at the splintering panels. 'Please…' she said.

The door disintegrated in a blizzard of sawdust. She saw her daughter in the jagged gap and began screaming.

Rachel's head was encased in a glistening ball of silver-black particles, an outsized globe that made her lurch drunkenly. It shifted like a drowsing swarm of insects, but the light behind her from the apartment windows glittered on metal. Rachel raised her hands and Banks saw they were gloved in the substance, tarry overflow dripping from her fingers.

Mrs Crofter was still screaming; Banks considered grabbing her shoulders, but found himself backing away as the misshapen figure in the doorway stumbled closer.

The air around Rachel shimmered and suddenly her hands were bare. A small cloud hung between mother and daughter for a moment, then flew the short distance to Mrs Crofter's head. As he watched, still edging along the corridor, it solidified into a mask. Mrs Crofter's screams were cut off and she fell without another sound; Rachel stood motionless, spherical head drooping to one side, as the body on the floor writhed. A few seconds later it stood up and both figures began demolishing the rest of the door.

Banks raced down the unlighted staircase. He'd seen something similar twice already, the first time in his parents' flat. After that, he supposed he could excuse himself on being lax about others' welfare; it wasn't an appropriate time to reflect, but he also supposed he'd always been selfish.

The idea came to him in the jump from one step to the next. Why hadn't it occurred to him sooner? He'd go to his brother.

Steve was at college in town. He was staying on in his hall of residence, likely to spend private time with his girlfriend. The hall was a new building, very secure, very well-insulated. Its sterile, shut-in air might be enormously valuable.

Assuming you get there, thought Banks. Assuming they let you in, or that there's even anybody left. Ignoring this with an effort, he waited to regain control of his breathing at the bottom of the stairs, then before doubt could cut in he went outside.

Emerging, he paused to study the crowds standing in the weak afternoon light. All of them had silvery, balloon-shaped heads without faces; none of them moved.

He took a very small step forward.

It started as an experiment in graphic design.

Banks had a weak grasp of science, not even a layman's understanding, and cared less. He'd followed the news as it developed, but without taking in the principles behind the technology; something to do with electrical impulses and magnets. Whatever started it, a privately-funded group had discovered the moving letters as a side-product of some industrial process – he wasn't sure, and besides, what did it matter? Tiny specks of alloy, stimulated somehow, became responsive to electric charges expressed as computer instructions. Once sensitised, they jostled and scurried along a metal surface and made words or pictures. Once sensitised, they couldn't be calmed down again.

The group believed there was a commercial application for this oddity; some eco-piety about cutting down on illuminated signs and billboards, if he remembered right. No more wasteful neon and poisonous, non-degradable ink; here was an emerging corner of the thrifty, self-sustaining, non-polluting future. The initial expenditure of power was slight, and then the particles recharged themselves with static – he'd read the explanation in a colour supplement and promptly forgotten the details. Of course, it didn't catch on; instead of a nice bright digital display announcing arrivals and departures, say, people had to watch insectile tendrils crawling across a blank surface and coalescing into words, rustling as they went; it was too creepy. Novelty alone wasn't enough, and despite an initial burst of worldwide sales the company had discontinued research; the secret couldn't be applied to anything heavier than the metal dust. They protested they'd made improvements, that the binding process was smoother and quicker. The alloy was no longer dependent on software, it was voice-responsive even – too late. Banks had never believed they really cared anyway; it was all a loss-leader, an extravagant advert for their other work. If so it succeeded; for a few months, the company prospered and gave little thought to disposal of its junked product.

Then the fragments became airborne.

Banks had been visiting his family. Not wanting to sleep in his younger brother's poky bedroom, he'd been using the sofa-bed and woken this morning with a slight hangover, a little later than intended. Just outside the room where he lay, he could hear a continuous, muted sobbing and a strange scraping noise. The sobbing sounded like his father.

Calling out got no response and Banks had hurried through a quick bathroom routine and got dressed before facing whatever was wrong, for which he was soon very glad. Selfish as ever: always putting his needs first, or so his parents liked to remind him. Perhaps as a result, it was rare that he saw them; this was a courtesy visit, under duress almost, and one he was regretting already – hence the hangover. The night before he'd caught up with old friends in town and everything had been a grey picture of pre-Christmas inertia, but perfectly normal. Now it was the weekend, and the street outside that should have been noisy and busy was silent. There was just the cloudy light glimmering on the balcony and his father sobbing in the next room. That and the grating, irregular sound he couldn't identify.

The old man was paralysed, in shock, and so for a while was Banks after he opened the door.

Seeing Banks, he'd jumped up and started blubbering incoherently about getting help, there'd been an accident. At first Banks couldn't understand what he was looking at. When he recognised the thing twitching and rolling on the kitchen floor under a carpet of seething flecks as his mother, he'd had to vomit in a corner.

Then the shimmering mass had extended its arms and dragged

his father in.

Since bolting from the room, Banks had hidden several floors below in an abandoned apartment. Looking out of the window, he'd seen the grotesque forms congregating on the pavement, straggling into the road until they almost filled the space. There was a gauzy, rippling haze over them, something like smoke but more active – as he watched, coils of the stuff streaked away in all directions, less like smoke now than clouds of gnats. He flashed on the kitchen window, wide open with the curtains stirring over his crouched father and the thing on the floor. Once the coldness and nausea passed, he thought he understood.

Below, flurries of the alloy whipped through the air, probing the buildings for open windows and new hosts. A wave of the stuff struck the glass by his head like a handful of gravel, and he'd cringed back with a shrill cry.

It was the intermittent slap of drifts against the pane and noises of movement somewhere that forced him out of the apartment. With some idea of finding other uninfected people, he'd begun a disordered, half-hearted search. Arriving on the floor below in time to see a woman he vaguely knew cornered shrieking at the far end and enfolded by what had been her husband, he'd run some more, and hidden some more.

The clouds of particles outside had eventually dispersed.

The infected were left standing in vague groups, but their stillness was total and seemed a solid, permanent thing. Banks had begun to think, to feel he might have a future beyond the gut-sinking numbness of the next few hours or minutes, but still he wanted company. He wanted a band of friends to run the gauntlet with; and all he'd found was Mrs Crofter, an acquaintance of his mother's.

None of the crowd reacted to his appearance.

With one hand on the half-open main door, ready to dart back inside, Banks watched for the slightest tremor of awareness – but they were all utterly immobilised, without even the faint activity of people standing at rest. The only movement was a breeze wafting over this maze of statues, vaguely tasting of pennies, subway trains; sweating, weak, he waited for the clouds of dust to seize him but none came. The tightness in his throat and chest loosened a little, and he took a single pace sideways on legs that felt close to crumpling.

Still no reaction.

Banks sidled another step, still close enough to the door to throw himself back if the figures twitched. Perhaps they'd suddenly all run at him in a great wall. Perhaps – Stop it, he told himself. But the image wouldn't go away; he stared at the mob until his eyes began to tingle and throw sparks over his vision. You're being stupid. Just because you're alone in the building… Ah, he countered, but he wasn't. That was the problem. Still, you've a better chance there than out in the open – there's food, you can lock yourself in, wait for help… But all morning, he hadn't heard a siren. The TV and radio in the deserted flat had been nothing but static, the internet disconnected, his mobile dead.

These calculations took a few airless, transfixed seconds. Banks looked at the street ahead, flocked with the distorted figures as far as he could see.

Then he half-turned and began inching his way backward through the door.

Once over the threshold, he heard a blurry sound somewhere overhead. Rigid, as if a hawser had tightened from his belly to his skull, he waited. There it was again – a stumbling of feet. Someone coming down the stairs.

Craning upward, Banks saw a hand sliding along the banister several floors above. He tried to relax his squeezed throat and call out, but stopped – the footsteps were clumsy, uncoordinated. Squinting into the shadows, he made out more of the shape coming down. There was something wrong with its head; he saw a silvery-grey blank where a face should be. As if sensing his attention, the thing began lolloping downward more quickly.

Banks crashed out into the freezing afternoon and hared along the street.

He waited for a start of alertness to pass through the crowd as he raced by, a clutching hand to take his shoulder.

The dormitory building was high and black in the winter light, its glass surface shot with captive gleams. Wind wrapped round him in blasts, hissing across the deserted car-park and smelling of space, of nothingness. The last of the infected stood frozen outside the chainlink fence, pressed to the wire; it groaned under their weight.

He was past telling himself that looking out for one wearing Steve's clothes was morbid.

There was a revolving door, airtight; he pushed through it into the lobby. The building was silent and heavy with vacancy, as were the twin greys of concrete and sky outside. Banks hurried up the stairs before fright could weigh him down.

Steve lived on the fourth floor; Banks met nobody and saw nothing on his way, racing up the stairs with a thick bloody taste growing in the back of his throat.

Steve's door was open, and the sight stopped him dead. Thoughtless and breathless, he stood with mouth hanging open and groped the wall for support, struggling with a renewed need to be sick. Through the door he could see an overturned table, books and papers spilled on the carpet.

The oblong of the double-glazed window, one that opened on an outward slant at the top, was ajar.

Banks regarded the opening with a neutrality beyond any feeling at all, barely registering a sudden stir in the air until a torrent of grey whipped against the sill and poured toward him.

With a hoarse scream, he slammed the door.

The hissing of the dust-cloud paced him along the outer wall.

After a blank interval, he came to himself gripping the stair rail high above the lobby and making a strange, asthmatic moaning noise. Through the glass of the revolving door he could see a grey blizzard whirling in the parking lot a few feet beyond, a vortex that waited just for him.

Strength and purpose seemed to bleed out of him with every tread back up the stairs.

Wish I'd bothered learning to drive, he thought – Left it a bit late.

It was getting dark. With the power off, shadows joined up to fill the corridors like rising water, swallowing detail; he found himself in a long passageway he couldn't be sure he recognised. One of the doors nearby was open a crack and he slammed it on reflex, but without urgency.

As the noise shot flatly down the passage, another door sprang open further along.

For a long time Banks and the girl watched each other, not speaking.

'I'm not a student,' he said at last.

'...Aren't you.'

It had been the first thing his exhausted mind could dredge up to break the silence, but he realised she was hovering in the doorway as if about to leap back into her room. It must have sounded odd; perhaps his voice and face were out of synch. Banks couldn't find the right response and wondered if some overloaded beam had snapped in his mind. He forced a smile. 'I came to see my brother. Steve Banks. But he's not here.'

'Steve?' Recognition crossed her face for a moment, then she flinched at some shock of memory.

'Oh, you know him then.'

The girl hadn't stopped studying him with a hard edge of wariness. She was slender, almost boyish, with a very thin pale face and a lot of straight, reddish-brown hair. Banks had never seen her before, although he'd spent as much time with his brother as he was able. Why couldn't she stop staring at him like that?

'Yes, I did know him. He's –'

'Not here, I know. Do you think anyone'd mind if I stayed in one of these rooms for a while? Just a few hours, I mean.'

'Steve's outside,' she said in a slow, careful voice. 'With the rest.'

'Oh.'

Again, his vagueness seemed to trouble her. She frowned, shaking her head without seeming to realise she did it.

He wanted to tell her it wasn't lack of feeling, he wasn't all selfishness, but maybe she was too young and righteous to understand. Then his stretched face began to ache and he found he was still smiling ingratiatingly.

'So what are you going to do now?' Her tone implied that was his concern alone.

Banks didn't know. He made an open-handed, confused gesture to stop the door's progress as she began to close it – he didn't want to be left on his own.

There was a furious rattling on the stairs.

They gaped at each other, like two people stunned by a realisation of love. The hollow, metallic slithering got closer, lost its echo – then the far end of the corridor disappeared in a curtain of grey. Banks watched it boil toward them with a feeling of overwhelming inevitability; after all, he'd been far too optimistic – in a building this size who knew how many ways inside there were? The girl had ducked into her room and the door was almost shut. Panicking, Banks jammed his heel and elbow against the shrinking margin and felt them crushed against the jamb. 'Don't!' he shouted. 'That's not fair! It's not fucking fair!'

With a convulsive shove he threw the door open, making her stagger back. He got a momentary glimpse of the room before she was trying to push him out again; her eyes were rolling back in her head with fear. She wasn't strong or heavy enough to force him out but as they scuffled in the doorway the cloud grew closer, so close he could see individual motes in a complex orbital dance as they arrowed toward his face.

'No time...' he pleaded.

She made to punch him and he caught her wrist, unbalancing them both; they tottered out into the corridor – then the cloud was upon them.

Banks swung her round and pushed her into it.

She screamed for a second, then silence. Banks heard the whisper of particles knitting around her head as he ran away.

Three floors up, he heard the whispering pursuit start again.

Looking wildly down into the stairwell he saw a veil of silver pass over the space below as the cloud streamed upward. Trailing after it came the girl, head sealed in its lumpen, sparkling crash helmet.

Sobbing, Banks scrambled up more flights of stairs, and more, until black X-ray jungles of veins seemed to flash in his eyes at each heartbeat. There was a door ahead and he blundered toward it with a feeling like drifting up and away from his own body – gasping, he burst into the cold air of the rooftop.

He was on a concrete field dotted with ventilators and skylights, the wind slicing into him. No way off the roof was visible, no convenient pipes or fire-escapes.

He looked at the green hills and woods visible around the town from this height, trying to frame a convincing thought that there was nothing more he could have done – no better place he could have run to. Then the clatter of something slipping under the door to the roof broke his concentration.

You're being pushed into a corner, he told himself, and you have to fight – he gathered his inner reserves to resist, to somehow repel, the cloud growing around him. Fight it.

But then he jumped.

Rushing toward the ground, he started to laugh: he could see it all.

It had started as an experiment in design – the words became airborne – the words became responsive. They snagged the anxieties of people everywhere.

As he fell, Banks saw the word spelled out past the car-park, replicated again and again across the town, maybe the world; he had to admire the moving letters. They had caught the mood, and crystallised it.

He plunged into a grey page with THE END written on it in human bodies, each head part of a letter, each letter part of a word scribbled over and over again as if in soft pencil; realising his trajectory would take him past the fence to where their pin heads spelled it out, he laughed harder. His landing would make a messy full stop.

'Form and function!' he shouted, air rushing into his mouth. 'That's *good* design!'

Then he hit the pavement.

PERIOD PIECE

Zoe came to a snap decision, the kind Pete loved; like the time she'd poked him on the shoulder at college, a stranger, and asked him to come out for a drink. 'Okay, in we go.'

'Sure?'

'Come on wussy,' she gave a pliant, sunny smile, 'I'll go first.'

Pete trailed after her. 'I'm not scared.'

'So you don't fear the dominating female. Female engulfment.'

'We'll wrestle later. Okay, let's look at death first – I s'pose it's like the cliché, sex and…' He reached in his pocket for cash. 'My treat.'

'Very romantic.'

'Death and the Maiden, darlin'.'

The Funeral Museum was small and poky, a nondescript grey building cramped between the Town Hall and a library. The interior came as a surprise; it had obviously been refurbished, recently and expensively. There were a lot of chrome and glass tables, low-slung chairs, and bright but diffused light lending warmth to the blue tiles everywhere. Seated behind the reception desk in the halo of a computer screen was a woman dressed in the same shade of blue, a small silver brooch like a crescent moon pinned to her lapel. Mid-thirties, Pete guessed, probably quite a fun and interesting lady to know behind the demure and coiffured official persona – she smiled, crinkling the corners of her eyes in an engaging way. She held his gaze for what seemed a long time before saying, 'Good afternoon,' in a quiet voice with a trace of foreign accent.

'We're here for the tour,' said Zoe, also smiling. She seemed to sense the same kind of warmth that Pete had.

'No tour. You can look around by yourselves, take your time.'

'Fabulous,' Pete said, stepping forward with cash. 'Two, please.'

The woman ignored his money and pushed two leaflets across the desk. 'No charge. Perhaps a small donation later. Here, look at these and I'll call someone to take you down.'

'Oh, right.' Pete joined Zoe on a sofa nearby, handing her a leaflet.

This Museum is dedicated to the habits and traditions associated with funerals of the 19th and 20th centuries, and contains genuine working exhibits. Infinity, plenitude, the Alpha and Omega – transience, transit, serenity.

There were a few blue-tinted pictures of hearses and coffins, black-plumed coaches, faded in beneath the text.

Eventually a morose, overweight man came and led them wordlessly past the reception desk. Pete didn't pause to study the office beyond; he got a glimpse of more blue tile, ranks of filing cabinets, rows and rows of desks all staffed by men and women talking briskly into headsets.

'What are they doing, then?' he asked the man's unshaven profile. 'Selling cemetery plots?'

'We'll go down in the lift,' the man grunted, breathing out half-metabolized alcohol. 'First, we'll see the coffin factory. Then I'll leave you to it.'

'Coffin – ?' blurted Zoe, 'they actually make them here?'

'Yes. All old men, downstairs, banging away at the coffins with their little hammers. All different-coloured coffins. Gold. Pink, even. Blue, of course. Very funny. You'll see.'

The light, the lift, his whole body, seemed to stutter and flicker.

In something called The Tyrannical Orange Book, he found a note which said –

"Yesterday's dreams seem as vital and relevant as last year's newspapers. Funny, that."

He didn't like the book and wanted to put it down, but it was getting dark and he couldn't find Zoe. Where had she wandered off to?

He turned the page and found an old photograph of himself, Zoe and some friends at college, all sitting in a bar. Their features kept changing somehow, were difficult to pin down. He felt great sadness looking at Zoe, who appeared very different to her real self.

On the next page she owned a large bear or dog – something like that – and they lived in a vast autumnal forest. The animal wandered off into the trees for a long time (days? Weeks?), and when it returned, loping slow and bedraggled down the path, it had a happy, faraway look, as if it had seen great things. It slumped limp and compliant against the hood of Zoe's car with a near-human grin.

In the same dense woods, a war began. Pete went away to fight, and was posted as a sentry in an outlying trench near a demolished cottage; he overheard the other soldiers placing bets on who'd be the first to get shot – he was favourite. He did die first, but had the satisfaction of being shown a crude diagram of the action in which his carping trench-mates were also killed by snipers.

Later, he walked with Zoe in a narrow alley of crumbling tenements and factories, beside a river choked with nettles. They laughed at the small shop they passed, where suits and masks were displayed on racks in the dusty window – Family Man and Woman with fatuous wooden features.

By the same river in fading sunlight, a man began to follow them through the railway-arches and overpasses. His face was very evil. Pete smashed a bottle he was carrying and wheeled round to confront the man; then he saw the man, too, held a broken bottle and was grinning.

Pete looked at a website that showed greyed-out footage of a dead woman on an autopsy table; as he watched, gloved hands cut her in half.

He had to write in the back of the book – to note down every chapel built on ley-lines and pagan sites; somehow he had to calculate it all exactly.

He was in the torchlit cellar of a vast cathedral. A robed shape advanced on him, arms stretched to ward him off, and he brandished a rusted hammer; the figure slipped back into darkness before he could strike it. He climbed mouldering steps into a white hall; there was a crowd of oddly-dressed people milling around in it, calling out in shrill voices – but he couldn't see Zoe anywhere. He called her name, then shouted it till it rang from the vaulted ceiling; the crowd rushed angrily toward him, still crying their nonsense. From among them came the King – a bewildered and impotent-looking youth, blonde, bearded and vacant; how could he justify himself to this playing-card figure?

He gathered himself to speak, to demand to know what they'd done with Zoe, but as he drew breath the King's courtiers all vanished – and then the hall vanished too, melting away. Behind the King was a dim city street at night. The King made a vague, despairing gesture and vanished in turn; Pete was left in the chill and wafting draughts of cars, crowds, with a feeling this had somehow happened before but without even an orange book to guide him.

MESSAGE (AN EPILOGUE)

A sheet of paper was slipped under my door one night. This is what it said.

"...how do you take revenge on a ghost? You can find the living person that most closely resembles it and kill that person of course, but that's a poor substitute and anyway it's not certain. A better way is to understand its existence in the hidden world, to pass through the Higgs Portal as it were, to take a new name, Eustache Goidel for instance, and cultivate new habits. Once you've done that you've broken its lock on you and can begin to track it – to be gallant and violent and stir up the blood. New name, new look, never be found. Then and ONLY then can the True Work begin. Things to note: Be careful of their hypnotic smell. Time your assassinations in unpredictable clusters. If you can't find your quarry, kill a person and make a fresh ghost. It should tell you what you need to know (and lose any wish to avenge itself) with the proper inducements – burnt offerings, blood, a year of your life etc. Either that, or fashion yourself a familiar. Kill a fox in the forest and split it with a stick, then wait till its heart rots green and small. Take that heart and its skull, skinned and washed clean in a stream. Bury them with the correct chemical compounds. A temporary creature should emerge from the ground after about a week – ask it whatever you need to know, then destroy it. This is a ruthless and thankless business we're engaged in. Take another new name, eg. Euphemia Hurlstone.

And remember, you have a right to be confused – you're only one of God's stray neurons, after all. It's tough, granted; but can also be an hedonic cascade, meteors of pleasure, when all goes well. I love my work despite everything, and so will you. And so you shall. You shall so.

Signed, A Friend."

I waited, but I haven't had another message yet.

previous publications

'It is Written' in The Second BHF Book of Horror Stories (BHF Books 2008)

'A Curse in Any Language' originally published in Arkham Tales #2 (Leucrota Press, February 2009)

'Perfectly Reasonable' in Estronomicon, Spring/Summer issue (Screaming Dreams, May 2009)

'Complaint from The Other World' in Murky Depths #9 (The House of Murky Depths, Sept 2009)

(Also performed by White Rabbit @ Are You Sitting Comfortably? The Basement, Brighton, December 2010)

(Republished by etherbooks.com as a download, October 2012)

'The Un-Explorers' in New Horizons #4 (BFS Publications, November 2009)

'Slaves of The Mummy' in The Third BHF Book of Horror Stories (BHF Books 2010)

'We Know Where You Live…' in Murky Depths #11 (The House of Murky Depths, February 2010)

'Bitten by the Birds of Paradise' in Estronomicon, Xmas issue (Screaming Dreams, December 2011)

'The Path Ends Suddenly' as a spoken-word audio track, Light Crude Records 2008 & 2012

'Lucky Bleeder' published by etherbooks.com as a download, January 2013

(Also performed by White Rabbit @ Are You Sitting Comfortably? Toynbee Studios, London, October 2012)

ABOUT THE AUTHOR

Matt Finucane is a British musician and writer.
www.mattfinucane.net